WITH YOU

A WITHOUT YOU NOVELLA

MARLEY VALENTINE

with
you

Copyright © 2025 by Marley Valentine

Cover design by PopKitty Designs
Photographer: WANDER AGUIAR :: PHOTOGRAPHY
Models: Jacob Cooley & Luke Schaeffer
Edited by Shauna Stevenson at Ink Machine Editing
Proofreading by Hawkeyes Proofing

This book contains mature content.

DEDICATION

To Julian and Deacon, you changed my life.

To everyone who has read, cried over, and loved Without You over the last five years, this book is for you.

I hope this glimpse into their life after the last page is everything you hoped for.

PART 1
THE WEDDING

DEACON

I know better than to wipe my sister's tears and ruin her makeup, but as they continue to fall down her cheeks, it looks like she's about to do a pretty good job of that herself. We're the only two remaining in the wedding suite, waiting for our cue to leave.

"These are h-happy t-tears," she manages to sputter out. "I promise. I j-just can't seem to m-make them stop."

"I can see that." Standing opposite one another, I place my hands on her shoulders and offer her a comforting squeeze. "Anything I can do to help? Do you want me to get Hayden?"

Her breath hiccups as she shakes her head, willing herself to stop. "I've already cried enough in front of him this weekend. The man deserves a break."

I narrow my eyes at her. "Have they been happy tears the whole time?"

"Of course," Victoria blurts out a little too quickly. "I'm just so happy for you and Julian."

There aren't many people in this world that I can read as well as I can read my sister. And while I know she isn't lying, I also know there are a million bittersweet reasons for her tears.

"You can tell me," I say gently, trying to coax out the words I know she doesn't want to say. "You know I feel it all too."

When she remains silent, I release my hold on her to search for a tissue. When I finally find the box, I grab it and hold it out to her. "Here," I say. "Wipe your tears and talk to me."

Appeasing me, she dabs at the corners of her eyes and then her nose, but she remains silent.

"You're not the only one who wishes he were here, you know," I confess to a quiet room. "But I can bet you're not selfishly torn up about what having him here would mean."

"Deac," Victoria whispers, immediately grabbing my hands and holding them between hers. "You know he would be happy for you."

Guilt lodges itself in my chest, threatening to sour what is meant to be the best day of my life. It's not about whether or not he would be happy for me, but rather the notion that my happiness is reliant on my brother's death.

It makes me feel selfish and indulgent.

It makes me feel unworthy.

It makes me feel like a thief.

"He's Rhett's."

Feeling overwhelmed, I allow myself to drop to the nearest couch and rest my head in my hands. My mother's words often creep into my conscience at the most inopportune times, twisting me up from the inside out.

It's been well over five years since we've spoken to one another, and while I have no doubt it's hard on my father and sister, the fact that I can still feel her hand on my cheek and the disappointment in her voice, even on my wedding day, I know my choice of self-preservation is the right one.

I can hear Victoria shuffle closer, then sit on the wooden coffee table in front of me.

She places a hand on each of my knees. "Is giving him up an option?"

The question rattles me, and I snap my head up to meet her gaze. "What did you just say?"

Her expression is sad and sullen. "I said, is giving him up an option?"

Confused, I shake my head. "Are you asking me, on my wedding day, if giving Julian up is an option?"

Victoria nods. "Yes," she answers resolutely. "Whatever you're feeling right now, would it go away if you gave him up? Would it all be less complicated if you gave him up?"

Shocked by her question, I straighten my spine. "You didn't think to ask me this when he and I first got together?"

"Then or now, is the answer different?" she challenges.

"No," I say, loud and irritated. "No. No. No."

I rise up off the seat, moving away from her, needing the space. "I don't even want to *think* about a life without him."

"Then don't," she says, so simple and matter-of-fact. "Only think about the life you have now. Not what could've or would've or should've."

Victoria grips the sides of her dress and raises the material up enough that she doesn't trip on her heels as she makes her way toward me. She stands opposite me and presses her palm to my chest, calming my racing heartbeat. "You and Julian are what are, and that is the only thing that matters."

I *know* that, I think to myself. I *know* that she's right, and six out of seven days in a week, I pay no mind to those heavy thoughts and I live in the moment. I love and allow myself to be loved, in a way that is beyond anything I could've ever dreamed up for myself.

A knock interrupts my wayward thoughts, and as if I needed proof that this man is tethered to me in every way possible, Julian's head pops through the open doorway, his eyes searching the room for me.

When that chocolate-colored gaze lands on me, the tightness in my chest eases immediately.

"What are you doing in here?" I ask, my eyes taking in the way he effortlessly fits into his tuxedo. "I thought we weren't supposed to see one another till the ceremony."

Victoria tries to sneakily slip outside as Julian crosses the threshold and approaches me. But before she disappears, I call out to her.

"Vic." She glances back at me over her shoulder. "I love you. Thank you."

"I love you too." Her gaze darts between Julian and me. "Both of you."

Curious, Julian's steps finally close the distance between us.

"What was that about?" he asks as he circles his arms around my neck. Ignoring his question, I press my mouth to his, needing to feel him, needing him to quiet the noise.

"Are you okay?" he murmurs against my lips.

Gripping his hips, I press him into me, needing him closer, needing the kiss to be deeper. As always, I need my body to say the words my mouth never can.

"I am now," I manage to croak out.

Guiding his hands up to my face, he reluctantly drags his lips away from mine and holds my gaze. "What is it?"

Closing my eyes, I try to hide my thoughts from him, try to stifle the emotion forever threatening to fall down my cheeks. I shake my head. "It's nothing you need to worry about."

"I thought after all these years you would know I'll always worry about you."

And I do know that. I know that nobody will ever come close to worrying, or caring, or loving me as much as this man does. His thumbs skate over my cheekbones, and I know he's patiently waiting for me to look at him. Despite knowing he'll see right through me, I do what I know he wants and let him see me; every thought, every fear, every flaw.

"I love you," he says the second our eyes meet.

My breath hitches at his unwavering devotion that, somehow, after all these years, still catches me off guard every single time.

"I love you too," I reply. "So much."

"Can you believe we're getting married today?" he whispers into the empty room. "You and me, husbands."

His eyes glisten with unshed tears, bright and beautiful, and so very content.

"Husbands," I whisper back. "Who would've thought?"

"Not me." A soft chuckle leaves his mouth. "But I've never been happier. You make me so happy, Deacon."

"I love you," I repeat, the three words never enough and yet all encompassing.

In sync, our mouths meet, and all the worry and confusion and hypotheticals from earlier fall to the wayside. The tragic beauty of our love sitting between us, like it always does, as sure and steady as the beats of our hearts, binding us together more than it ever has before.

There's a reason we don't have eyes on the backs of our heads, because we can't look back. We can't change the past, we can only live in the moment.

Here and now.
Him and me.

JULIAN

Our hold on one another tightens and our kiss morphs from connection to desperation very quickly. Whatever was bothering Deacon is no longer at the forefront of his mind.

I can feel myself harden behind my pants as his tongue snakes out to meet mine, tasting and taking.

"Deacon," I breathe out. "We need to stop."

He presses his own length against mine. "You should've thought about that before you came in here. What did you expect to happen?"

"I missed you," I confess. "It was a dumb idea."

His mouth trails kisses across my jaw and down my neck while his hand slips between us and cups my erection. "We could've taken care of this before the day even started." He squeezes, and I groan. "More than once."

"I'm sorry," I say. "I'll do better next time."

"Next time," he balks, rearing his head back, moving his lips away from mine. "Do you plan on doing this again?"

"Only with you," I answer before recklessly kissing him again. "Five years. Ten. Twenty. Fifty."

"If you don't walk out of this room right now, we're going to be late to our own wedding," he warns as I rock my hips into his hand. "And I won't be even a little bit sorry."

Groaning, I place my hands on his chest and push myself off of him. The distance between us already making me ache.

We stare at one another, for the first time finally allowing ourselves to truly look at each other. Taking in the magnitude of what we're both wearing and what we're about to finally do. Deacon is dressed in a navy blue suit, with black lapels and a black bow tie. I thought there was nothing better than my fiancé, the mechanic, coming home covered in oil and grease, with a white t-shirt stretched over his beautifully defined chest, but this might just be the winner.

Because this is all for me.

"You look breathtaking," I admit.

"You like?" he teases.

"I love."

"You don't look too bad yourself," he teases, stepping toward me.

"Don't." I hold up my hand. "My self-control is non-existent right now."

Smirking, Deacon bats my hand away and stands in front of me, reaching for my bowtie. "Don't worry," he says, untying it and tying it back up. "I'll make tonight worth the wait."

When he unties it a second time, I raise a brow at him. "What are you doing? I thought I did it right."

"It was perfect. I'm just finding ways to be close to you."

His admission is soft, and his touch tender as his fingers graze my neck. "Are you sure you're okay?" I ask, bringing the conversation back to whatever was bothering him when I walked into the room.

"I think he'd be happy for us," he says, completely throwing me off my axis.

Emotion lodges itself in the back of my throat, words failing me. Instead, my eyes fill with tears, easy to form and quick to fall.

We don't talk about Rhett much. Not in reference to our relationship, but rather as a separate entity. A brother, a boyfriend, a best friend. But he very much exists in everything we do and every choice we make.

The guilt ebbs and flows, for both of us, but our love for one another always overrides it.

"I know he would," I assure him, keeping my voice steady. "He wanted nothing more than for us to be happy."

"And I am so happy," Deacon says, his voice laced with awe.

His hands straighten my bowtie one last time before he drops a gentle kiss to my lips. Stepping back, his arms fall to his sides, his blue eyes watery and filled to the brim with nothing but reverence for me.

"You're ready now," he says confidently.

"I know," I say with a smile. "Now, hurry up and make me your husband."

STRAIGHTENING MY SPINE, I button up my tuxedo jacket, and breathe through the anticipation that's fluttering around in my stomach as I take in the room before me.

Our wedding was always going to be a small, intimate event, Deacon's family and the few friends we have accumulated along the way. Both perpetual loners, it's very easy for us to get sidetracked in our bubble, but when we let people in, it's always a pleasant reminder, especially for Deacon, of just how much love there is in the world.

To give and receive.

Dressed to the nines, Wade squeezes my shoulder as I reach the end of the aisle. Both Deacon's best man and our self-appointed marriage officiant, even though the decision was made when we were all heavily intoxicated, there really is nothing more perfect than the person who has supported us the most, marrying us today.

"Are you ready?" he asks.

"Are you?" I retort back. "Did you practice all your lines?"

He raises a bunch of folded papers. "I did, but I bought these as a backup."

"Who would've thought it would be hard to officiate a wedding," I tease.

"Harder than getting the license, that's for sure."

This makes us both laugh.

"Are you nervous?" Wade asks me. "Do you have your vows ready?"

I tap my temple. "I've got it all up here."

"Show off," he mutters.

Before either one of us gets the chance to say another word, Adele's "Make You Feel My Love" starts to play on the speaker, and the flutter of anticipation returns to the pit of my stomach.

It doesn't matter that we've already seen one another, touched and spoken to one another. It doesn't matter that a million 'I love you's' have already left my mouth for this man, and my lips have kissed him an endless number of times. Because nothing in existence could've prepared me for the way I would feel, watching Deacon walk down the aisle, arm in arm with his father, toward me.

Toward *me*.

An overwhelming sense of warmth fills me from head to toe. My love for him and his love for me; it overflows, spilling between us, drowning us in the best way possible.

They hold on to one another tightly, each of their steps still seemingly too far away.

I want them to hurry, I want Deacon close.

I want to make him my husband.

Bill Sutton is a stoic man I have known almost my whole life. I've seen him experience the worst things a parent can endure, and yet I have never seen him as overcome with emotion as he is right now.

The years have aged him, lines at the corners of his eyes, deep creases on his upper lip, proof that despite his denial, he has reacquainted himself with his love for tobacco these last few years. I know the tug-o-war between his remaining son and his wife has taken its toll, but even through the stream of tears that fall down his face, the pride and happiness he has for Deacon in this moment is unmissable.

When they finally reach the end of the aisle, Bill releases Deacon, just to hold his face in his hands and stare at his son. As they wordlessly stand there, in front of each other, I take in what is the history and the future of the Sutton family. They've been through a lot together since Rhett died, but they've worked harder at their relationship than I think either one of them ever expected, and today is proof that none of that hard work has gone to waste.

Bill kisses Deacon on the forehead before taking a step back. But when I expect him to move to the side, he surprises me by stepping forward and holding my own face in his hands.

"I'm so happy for you, son," he says, his eyes full of unshed tears. "I'm so unbelievably happy for you both."

Unable to contain the onslaught of emotions, I wordlessly nod through my own tears at the man who never once questioned taking me under his wing. Opening his heart and family to me all those years ago, single handedly changing the trajectory of my life, making sure I knew I was welcome, I was wanted. I was loved.

And now here I am, ready to profess my undying love to his son. Because Deacon is welcome, he is wanted, he is loved.

Releasing his hold on me, Bill grabs Deacon's hand and places it in mine.

"I love you both," he says firmly.

"I love you, Dad," Deacon manages to whisper. "Thank you."

Bill squeezes our shoulders and moves himself to the side, outside the aisle and to a seat beside Victoria. When everyone's seated, I bring my gaze to Deacon and lace my fingers with his.

"Hi," he says softly.

"Hi."

"Ready to get married?" he asks.

Offering him a wink, I turn my head to Wade and give him a subtle nod.

Smiling back at me, our officiant and best friend straightens his back, standing proudly, as he brings the microphone to his mouth. "Friends. Family. Welcome to the wedding of Deacon Sutton and Julian Reid."

DEACON

Unintentionally, I drown out Wade's voice, my attention too focused on Julian; enraptured with the man before me. Dressed in all black, his tuxedo fits every inch of him like a second skin, his satin bowtie now perfectly placed at the base of his throat. His hair is slicked back, and despite his red-rimmed eyes, I don't miss the smile stretched across his face or the flush of his cheeks.

Happiness radiates off him, and I try to breathe through the tight feeling in my chest. Between missing Rhett, gratitude for my father and sister, and the absolute disbelief that I get to live the rest of my life loved by a man like Julian, it's almost too much for my heart to contain.

There have been many times in my life when I've sat amongst the crowd, happy to remain quiet and go unnoticed. For the most part, the background is where I enjoy being. Little or no attention is perfect.

My house. My bubble. My man.

But like all of our life-changing moments, today, with all of our friends and family watching me, I don't care about all the attention. I'll stand here boasting about and praising the best man there is till my voice is hoarse and my legs give out.

Julian's hands squeeze mine, and I find myself matching his wide smile. It's almost impossible to contain the jittery feeling inside my stomach, my patience waning, wanting to race ahead to the part where we say "I do" sooner rather than later.

"I have known Deacon my whole adult life," I hear Wade say. "And I have never seen him happier than he's been these last five and a half years. I have never seen him fuss and fawn the way he does over Julian."

A low rumble of laughter sweeps through our guests as Wade continues talking. "I've had the pleasure of having a man like Deacon by my side; my best friend, my business partner, my brother. I've borne witness to him in every stage of his life, and by far this has been the best one."

Wade pauses, clearing his throat, visibly trying to avoid getting too emotional in front of an audience. "Life can be tricky," he continues. "There are real highs and even worse lows, but with Julian by his side, these two together know how to weather a storm.

"Julian and Deacon, it is an honor to be able to celebrate your love and your union, and I know I'm not the only one here today who feels this way."

Wade gestures to my sister, who is once again dabbing at her eyes with a tissue. Victoria rises up off the seat and makes her way to the nearby lectern. Instead of asking Victoria to go the traditional route and read a romantic poem or sonnet, Julian and I told her she had free rein to speak from the heart.

"Hi," she says nervously into the microphone. "I'm just going to go ahead and warn everyone that there will be tears, and please just bear with me."

Everyone laughs.

"For those of you who don't know, Deacon and I had a brother, Rhett. And he died almost seven years ago."

Her words stun me, especially after our earlier conversation, and I feel my hands instinctively tighten around Julian's. His gaze bores into mine, reassuring me, because he knows without the exact words just how muddled up I can sometimes feel inside. But I trust him. Holding his gaze, breathing in and out, I give my fears and anxieties to the man I love, because I trust him to take care of me when I need it most.

And like all those years ago, when we were navigating our initial feelings, I trust us.

I trust what we have, what we've built, and what we've promised.

Implicitly.

"Unfortunately for Rhett, he knew the end was near," Victoria continues. "So in his free time, he wrote us all some letters."

My heart begins to thump erratically in my chest, and tears fill my eyes as I reminisce on my letter and all the things he wrote to me. Julian's smile turns a little sad, and I know he's thinking about his own letters and his own choices.

As if he can read my mind, he offers me a subtle shake of his head and leans forward, quickly whispering in my ear, "I don't regret a single thing."

"*I love you,*" I mouth just before we both tune back in to Victoria's speech.

"As one would expect, there was a long list of things Rhett asked me to do, as the oldest sibling. Some were funny and ridiculous. And some..." Vic's voice cracks as she continues. "And some broke my heart," she confesses. "And some, on a day like today, almost feel prophetic."

Victoria turns her body to face Julian and me, careful not to drop her gaze or lose the connection. As she starts speaking again, I realize she's no longer reading from the page, because she's memorized the words.

For this moment, or because she's read it so many times, I don't know.

"On a serious note," Vic starts, and I realize she's jumping straight into the part of the letter she wants to share. "Everything in this letter is just a guide, it's an option, because who am I to tell you how to live your life? I barely lived mine." She pauses, because I know not everyone understood Rhett's dark humor. "But there is one thing that isn't negotiable."

Victoria's familiar eyes dart between us before she says, "Deacon and Julian need one another. I know there's distance and animosity and a whole lot of love lost between them."

I hear the words in her pause loud and clear.

Because of Mom.

"But they are two of the best people I know, and I wish they knew that about themselves. I wish they knew that grief is easier shared, and that moving forward doesn't always mean they can't sometimes look back.

"I'm here. I'll always be here. For all of you. Cheering you on. Wishing I was there. Kiss Lia for me. Love you, Vic. Love you all."

The sob that wrenches itself out of my mouth surprises me the most. I tug my hands from Julian's hold and bury my head in them instantly.

My shoulders shake as I struggle to regulate my emotions. It isn't shame or embarrassment, but just the overwhelming sensation of being taken care of and understood, in a way I was never able to experience when he was alive.

The uncertainty from earlier shifts into that familiar, ever-present coexistence of grief and gratitude.

I feel firm arms circle my body and lips against my neck. It isn't often I allow myself to fall apart, and I never would've chosen for it to happen today, in front of everyone. But hearing those words out of Victoria's mouth and knowing what Rhett had asked of me in my letter, I can't help but wonder what he saw that we didn't.

He was so certain and so sure. And that's more than enough for me.

It solidified what I so often knew, but regretfully allowed myself to be insecure about.

This is right. Julian and I are right. And everyone here in this room knows it too.

As my tears subside, and my breathing steadies, my arms make their way around Julian. Hugging him to me, my head nestles in the crook of his neck. As always, he is my comfort and my rock, patient as ever, making sure I'm okay.

Slowly, I lift my head up and meet Julian's tear-filled eyes.

"I promise, we will get married at some point today," I joke.

"You know I'll wait," he says, the softest, most beautiful smile painted on his face.

He presses his lips to mine, comforting me when Wade's hands land on our shoulders, pulling us apart. "No kissing, folks, we still have some vows to get through."

Knowing what's coming next, I don't even bother wiping my eyes. Feeling a lot more exposed and vulnerable than I expected, I know it won't be an easy feat to get through my vows without breaking down again.

Inhaling, I steady my breath and just bask in the occasion. Even with the inundation of tears, emotions and confessions, I know this is a once-in-a-lifetime moment. Everything we've endured and experienced has led us here. Every step, every fight, every apology.

Every single time I said I love you.

"And because I'm certain we all want to cry again, it's time for these two gentlemen to exchange their vows," Wade says, steering the ceremony back on track.

Everyone laughs, and as they do, I grab Julian's hands in mine, my only focus, him. I tighten my hold and try to ignore my quickening pulse, hoping that all the nights I spent, pen to paper, writing and rewriting, memorizing and reciting—over and over again—was enough.

Glancing at Wade, he offers me a nod, and I take it as my cue. A blanket of silence falls over the room, and I feel the air tightening around us, closing us in, both of us back in our bubble.

Locking eyes with Julian, I let his brown depths soothe and comfort me as I try to swallow past the lump of emotion lodged in my throat.

Filled with love and adoration, I focus on the man in front of me, and prepare to proudly profess my love for him.

"Julian," I say on an exhale. "Julian. Julian. Julian."

His mouth ticks up in a smirk, and all the knots of tension and anxiety loosen instantly.

I've got this.

"I love you," I say simply. "It's funny how easy those words are to say now. In fact, they almost never feel enough. I can remember when those words first left my mouth..." My voice trails off as I remember those hours in that hotel room, the tears, the sweat, the sex—the love between us and just how life changing those three words became.

"I hadn't really felt love before you," I continue. "Not in that all-consuming way."

Pulling my hands away from his, I raise them to his cheeks, cupping his jaw. "And you consume me, Julian. My whole world is you, and there isn't a single thing about that I want to change."

I catch the tear that falls from his lashes with my thumb, and talk directly to him.

From my heart to his.

JULIAN

"Falling in love with you..." Deacon shakes his head. "I never saw it coming. I never saw *you* coming. But there you were, so open and honest and vulnerable, all the things that were so foreign to me; all the reasons that made me want to stay. In your orbit, in your life. Once I had you by my side, there was nowhere else in this world I wanted to be."

Needing to touch him, I place my hands over his as he continues. "You're patient and kind and protective. Protective of me." His cheeks turn a shade of red as he admits, "And I never thought myself worthy of protecting."

Staring at one another, we both sit with his revelation, no doubt both of us back at his parents' place, reliving a pivotal moment in our relationship.

"On paper we are nothing more than roadblock after roadblock after roadblock. But in reality?" I watch a smile filled with confidence and adoration stretch across his face, despite his unshed tears. "In reality, loving you is living."

My chest tightens as I let those words soak into my skin and settle in my bones. Life had been so bleak and hopeless before him, and without even trying, he brightened up my days and shined light on my future.

"And I want to do both—love you and live with you," he says with certainty. "Your love has healed me, Julian. And I want to spend the rest of my life saying thank you."

On instinct I shake my head and mouth the word "no" because we both know there is nothing to thank me for. Unperturbed by my outburst, Deacon just nods and holds me tighter.

"Yes," he insists. "I want to love you, the way you deserve, till my dying breath. Every minute of every hour, of every day, I promise to make you feel my love."

Gently releasing our hands, Deacon steps back and glances at Wade, who, right on cue, holds out my ring, a brushed white gold band that Deacon and I chose together, his engagement ring now sitting on my right hand.

Butterflies swarm my stomach as I hold out my left hand to him. For five and a half years we have lived and built a life together, like we're already married. And yet the idea of being tied to him in one more way, has my blood pumping and my heart racing.

It feels like the sun rising on a brand new day, anticipating what's to come and what our life will be. What it'll be like to wake up forty years from now, beside him, still needing him, still wanting him, still loving him.

"Julian," Deacon says, rerouting my focus back to him. "When I fell in love with you, I was gifted a world where shame and heartache don't exist. I found a world where being myself is more than enough."

My gaze falls to his throat, watching the way it bobs as he searches for whatever words he wants to say next.

"I love you, Julian Reid." His voice is laced with conviction and emotion as he slides the ring down my finger. "I promise to love you when it's quiet and love you when it's loud. I promise to love you in the light and in the dark. When you need me and even when you don't."

"There isn't a world or a lifetime where I won't need you," I interject, not caring about the order or the formalities or anything else but making today about him and my love for him.

"I guess I'll love you in every world and every lifetime, then, huh?"

He brings my hand up to his lips, kissing my newly adorned finger, his gaze never leaving mine. "It's you and me. Always."

I can feel everything around us slipping away as we both get lost in the moment, as I get lost in his declarations. And I momentarily wonder why we didn't just do this without an audience, where I didn't have to wait to say how I felt, where I could reassure him that loving him has been the easiest thing I've ever done in my life. Where I could kiss him and touch him, showing him all the ways just how perfect he is.

When Wade taps me on the shoulder, I realize I missed his introduction to say my vows.

"Sorry," I say quickly.

He smiles and shrugs. "It's your show, man, take all the time you need."

Uncharacteristically, I find myself shaking my legs and arms out, like I'm warming up for a race. It has all our guests chuckling and Deacon smiling at me, unperturbed, taking me as I am, in any moment.

"Do we think I can say these without crying?" I ask jokingly, knowing it'll be very much impossible.

Deacon offers me a smirk. "It'd be nice if I'm not the only one."

Slipping my hand inside my jacket, I pull a folded post-it note from the inside pocket, open it, and scan the words scrawled on there in my messy handwriting.

Quickly, I fold it back up and then slip it inside Deacon's suit jacket instead of mine. In a swift movement, he grabs my hand, brushing his lips across the back before pressing a kiss to my skin.

Even with the softest touch, electricity races through me, never tiring of the affection this man effortlessly showers me with.

He guides our hands between us and we interlace our fingers, my gaze getting caught on my wedding band sitting beautifully between us.

Staring at the sight a little too long, I eventually clear my throat and bring my gaze back to Deacon's. My broody man is no longer broody, not today anyway. The lightness in his blue eyes unmissable, his smile soft, his expression at ease.

"Deacon," I breathe out. "You were under my skin before I even knew it. You took care of me before either of us knew that's what you were doing or what it even meant."

My hands tighten in his as my eyes well with tears. "You say I'm the protector, but you always protect me. You aren't a fighter by nature, but time and time again I have seen you fight for us." The handle I have on my emotions slowly starts to slip, the shake in my voice evidence. "You have sacrificed for us," I manage to breathe out. "You have lost because of us."

Quickly, I raise my arm and slide my face against the material, trying to catch tears before they fall.

"And I know there have been times it's been bittersweet and painful," I continue. "But you make sure I know our life together is worth it.

"There aren't enough words in the English language to convey just how grateful I am for you choosing me, for loving me and allowing me to love you." I bring our interlaced hands to my lips and kiss his fingers. "You continue to be the steady rhythm of my heartbeat. You are worthy and you are special, and I've never been more grateful to call someone mine."

In my peripheral I see Wade holding out Deacon's ring, waiting for me to take it. When I have the circle-shaped jewelry in between my fingers, I stretch and straighten Deacon's hand and then slide the ring down.

"I promise to love you always and unconditionally," I tell him. "In the good times and the bad times. But I promise to love you the most when we're knee deep, too busy, and messily wading through everything in between.

"I love you, Deacon. You own me," I choke out. "My heart is yours till the day you say you don't want it anymore."

And just like all those years ago, Deacon shakes his head, face streaked with tears. Stepping closer to me, he raises his hands to cradle my face.

"Never," he says hoarsely. "I will never not want you."

Beyond impatient, my own hands mirror his and I bring him to my waiting mouth. Relief sweeps through me as his lips meld to mine, the kiss a sweet, relaxed exhale.

Somewhere in the background I hear Wade announce us as husbands, and all our friends and family cheering in unison, but all I can focus on is him.

All I *want* to focus on is him.

Settling into the kiss, I don't care if it's supposed to be a peck or if everyone gets tired of watching. I drop my hands from his face and wrap my arms around his neck. On instinct, Deacon's arms circle my waist, our bodies now flush against one another.

The kiss picks up in pace, soft and gentle morphing into deep and determined. It's our past and our present and our future. It's the flutter of anticipation in my stomach, and the heat swimming in my veins. It's every exchanged promise, every loud declaration, every hard earned moment of our love.

It's him and me.

Julian and Deacon.

"Husbands," he murmurs against my lips.

Smiling, I echo, "Husbands."

DEACON

"Are you hiding?"

Turning his head in my direction, my father removes the cigarette from his mouth. "Figured you'd call me when you needed me."

Crossing the threshold, I step out onto the small alfresco area attached to the side of our reception venue and lower myself to the wooden bench beside him.

Sidling up to him, I nudge his shoulder. "Are you okay?"

His brows knit together. "Why wouldn't I be?"

I shrug, not really having an answer but wanting to check in on him nonetheless.

"That was a lot of crying you did back there at the ceremony," I tease.

A husky chuckle leaves his mouth. "I don't recall you holding yourself together any better than I did."

We're so alike, Dad and me, that it feels like more than a coincidence that we've both been on our own road trip of self-discovery at the same time.

"Thank you for coming today, Dad," I say. "I know how ha—"

His hand squeezing my knee silences me. "Today is your day, Deac. You don't need to mollycoddle or worry about me."

He says it as if it were easy, as if these last five years seeing him without my mother didn't make me feel like a selfish prick, every. Single. Time.

After choosing to go no contact with her, I learned that she and my father had separated. With every intention to repair their marriage and deal with their grief, I know his side of the journey. But the unspoken rule about my mother, as a person, as the person who has hurt me the most, I don't ask and they don't tell.

"According to Julian, I do that," I say. "Worry about the people I love."

"I love you too, son," he says, patting my knee. "I'm so honored to be here, seeing you and Julian as grown men." The last word gets lost in a shuddery breath, and I don't need to guess why. "I'm just basking in it all," he admits. "There's a lot of peace that comes with knowing your kids are happy and loved."

"Are you happy and loved, Dad?" I find myself asking him before I even have a chance to process just how hard this question might be for him to answer.

"I am," he says quicker than expected. Surprising me, he stands up, and I follow suit until we're facing each other.

Large, firm hands settle on my shoulders. "Life didn't go at all how I expected it to, and I know I'm not an anomaly or unique, and there are many people in this world who have endured the same or worse than me, but today, sitting here with you, I don't hate where it's led me.

"I think happy and loved look different for me at this stage of my life, but I'm good here."

Eyes like mine, just older and wiser, hold my stare as my

chest tightens at his honesty. Empathy and understanding settle between us.

"Thank you, Dad."

Wordlessly, he pulls me to him, hugging me close. There's no rush in our embrace, all the things we've shared, out loud and in silence, alone and together.

"I love you, Deacon."

"Love you too."

"What's this?" Victoria's question interrupts the moment, but my face splits into a smile at the sound of her voice. "Did I miss the family meeting?"

Turning, I extend an arm out to her. "You're just in time."

She huddles between Dad and me as we both wrap our arms around her. "Seriously though, what did I miss?"

"Your brother thinks now that he's married and a huge sap, that we all have to be."

"Hey," I say in mock defense.

"Says the man who was crying while walking Deacon down the aisle," Vic teases, and the three of us laugh.

It feels good to be like this with my family, the mood light and the three of us joking and enjoying the day, despite the unavoidable onslaught of emotions. Even though the focus of the day is on Julian and me, I love how in this moment we can talk so freely, about anything.

We're proof that we're constantly living and learning. We're growing and evolving, the perfect example of how possible it is to be both hurt and happy.

"I hate to break this up," Victoria eventually says, "but your husband is looking for you. He's waiting to dance with you."

My husband.

I feel my grin widen at his new title, knowing the elation at hearing it would never cease.

"I'll meet you inside," I tell them both, my feet moving before the words have even left my mouth, desperate to get to my *husband*.

The thought of Julian waiting for me, knowing that this dance is one step closer to our night together and our honeymoon, has my heart racing. I would never get enough of him. It's just that simple. Being in his presence, breathing the same air, waking up in the same bed. It doesn't matter what we're doing, as long as it's together.

Walking back into the reception hall, I'm expecting Julian to be talking to a few guests, milling around in a group somewhere waiting for me.

What I don't expect is him in the middle of the room, hands in his pockets, casually waiting for me. Tux jacket back on, he looks as handsome and radiant as ever, his features content, his body language relaxed.

Smiling at me, he extends an arm out, calling me to him, guiding me into his arms, welcoming me home. As I place my hand in his, the music begins to play, and I let him lead me around the dance floor.

The sound of Dermott Kennedy's "What Have I Done" fills the room, the lyrics hitting me just as hard this time as they did the first time I heard them. I'm not an avid music listener and can't keep up with things that are popular and trendy, but every now and then the right song finds me.

"Who knew this whole time, all I had to do was ask you to marry me and you would dance with me," Julian teases.

"You know I'm awful at it," I answer. "I've got two left feet."

Julian presses his hand into the side of my torso. "Lucky we practiced, then."

"I wasn't going to pass up the opportunity to dance with you in our living room every night this week," I confess.

"All you ever have to do is ask."

I know he meant it beyond just dancing in the living room. Our life up until tonight has been proof of that, it isn't just in the words, but always in his actions. There is no doubt he would give me the world, even without me asking.

And even though it's more than reciprocated, the inner voice sometimes gets the better of me. My insecurities understanding why I want to give him everything, but not believing I deserved it in return.

"How long do you think before we can ditch this party?" Julian asks, and the unexpected question has me laughing out loud.

"I thought I was the only one thinking that," I reveal.

He tips his head to the side. "I am very much ready to take this party elsewhere. Somewhere a little more private, if you know what I mean."

I subtly press myself against him, knowing it would take little to no time for my body to react. "Just say the word and your wish is my command."

Dancing ceases as eager lips find mine, his mouth wordlessly telling me exactly what he wants. Moving my hands to his face, I kiss him soft and slow, trying to tame our insatiable need. While kissing him is always familiar and safe, I could feel the exhilaration of the day skirting around the edge of every touch.

It feels new and elevated, in a way I hadn't anticipated, because while we were living like a married couple up until this point, it was the big "fuck you" to anyone who ever doubted us that fueled the fire.

The music changes, and our guests fill the dance floor, but even air can't get between us. If it isn't our mouths pressed together, it's our foreheads, our gazes locked. I'm lost in his chocolate-colored eyes with nothing but the future mapped out in front of me.

With him by my side, I can see the bigger house, the lifelong friends, and a family. In his eyes, I see the life neither of us thought we were worthy of, but a life that we would cherish and protect, above all else. Together.

DEACON

"Hurry," Julian murmurs against my lips.

"I'm trying," I say, biting his bottom lip. "But I'm too distracted."

He slips his hand between us, grazing my thickening length, and I groan into his mouth. "We're going to end up naked in this hallway if you don't stop that."

"I'm sure everyone will enjoy the show," he taunts.

At the sound of the beep, I hurry us into the hotel room, Julian's hands now gripping my waist as I guide us both to the bed in the center of the room. Allowing myself to fall back onto the mattress, I expect Julian to climb on top of me, but instead he steps out from between my legs and gazes down at me, eyes filled with love, yet his expression is reserved.

"What's wrong?"

He shakes his head, the side of his mouth tipping up into a small smile. "Nothing."

I readjust my straining erection. "Then why aren't you on this bed with me? I thought after you mauling me in the elevator, this is where we were headed."

"Oh," he says with a nod, "we're definitely still headed there."

I raise a brow at him. "But?"

"Not a but," he says, shaking his head. "More like a *holy shit, we did it.*"

Chuckling, I rise off the bed, stepping toward him. "No regrets, then?"

There's no seriousness in the question, and yet I feel myself waiting with bated breath for an answer I already know.

"About marrying you?" He shakes his head vehemently. "Absolutely not."

"And the day?"

Arms circle my neck as he places kisses against my jaw. "Perfect."

Angling my head, I give him access to the length of my neck, the heat between us rising with every press of his mouth.

"I'm going to have a shower," he says in between kisses. "Want to join me?"

Before I have the chance to answer, Julian steps back and strips out of his tuxedo jacket, haphazardly throwing it onto the floor. Deft fingers reach for his bow tie, sliding it off his neck and then undoing the top button of his shirt.

My eyes stay glued to his hands as they move down his body, exposing his skin to me inch by agonizing inch.

My cock is hard, my mouth is desperate, my body aching for him.

His shirt falls to the floor, and my groan echoes off the walls. Next is his belt, followed by the button of his pants. Watching him slide the zipper down to expose his briefs almost feels like torture.

We've gained a lot of confidence in the bedroom over

the years. Both of us in different ways and for different reasons. There should've been a discomfort about being with a man for the first time, and I'd waited for it, almost wanting it.

But it never came.

Instead, there was disbelief that something so new and foreign and unexpected could feel so perfect.

I've never felt more like myself than I have with Julian, and our compatibility and chemistry together solidifies that even more. When you're with your best friend, there is no embarrassment, shame, or awkwardness. Sex can be both fun and absolute fire; we can lust and laugh all in the same breath.

Not wanting to be left behind, I begin taking off my own clothes, mirroring his movements, less than a minute behind. My gaze dances over every inch of his naked skin, seeing the way he's filled out over the years. It isn't just about spending more time on himself but finding himself worthy to be taken care of. Prioritizing himself; his wants and needs.

I drag my gaze down the smattering of hair on his torso, to the V-cut of his abdomen, and feel my own cock thicken painfully at the sight of his hard length resting beautifully against it. He takes measured backward steps toward the bathroom, all while his gaze is on me. I stalk toward him as each item of my clothing falls to the floor.

Stretching his arms across the doorway, a cocky, teasing smirk spreads across his face. His whole demeanor screams "catch me if you can," and catching him is exactly what I plan on doing.

"You're still wearing too many clothes," he says, glancing down at my underwear.

"Want to do something about it?"

His hands slip beneath the waistband of my boxers, and he pushes them down, my cock slapping my stomach in the process. Raising his eyes to meet mine, Julian watches me as he kneels on the floor and slides them down my legs before I step out of them.

Lightly grazing the length of my body with his fingers, Julian's smirk reappears as he bypasses my aching cock and slowly rises to his feet.

I raise my brow. "Better?"

Nodding, he returns to his position in the doorway, his expression almost challenging me.

Wordlessly accepting it, my hands land on his chest, his muscles under my palms, my thumbs grazing his nipples.

Julian's breath hitches, and I revel in his reaction.

Lowering my head, I kiss the length of his collarbone and up his jaw before gently pushing him past the threshold. When his backside hits the cabinet, I turn him around so we're both staring at our reflections in the mirror.

Our gazes meet as I press my hard length against his naked ass, the heat from earlier reigniting. Julian tips his head back with a groan, and my hand rounds his hip and circles his thick erection.

The skin is hot and tight around his shaft, the tip of his cock glistening and peeking out. I move my hand up and down as I pepper his shoulders with open-mouthed kisses, my eyes never leaving our reflection.

"Did you think you were the only one who could tease?" I say against his skin. "Look at us in the mirror, baby."

Lowering his head, I feel the deep inhale, his back to my front, as his eyes take us in. With my mouth resting on his shoulder, our eyes boring into one another, I drag my free hand up his torso and rest it possessively around his neck.

I guide my tongue over his fluttering pulse as my hand moves up and down his shaft, stroking him painfully slow. He tries to piston his hips, and I know his body well enough to know he wants more. Wants my hand to grip him tighter, my hand to jerk him faster.

"Not so fast," I tell him. "I want you to feel the absolute torture it's been all night to keep my hands off of you."

My movements purposefully still on his cock, and I squeeze it while my mouth kisses up and down the nape of his neck. Absolutely enthralled by the idea of edging him, my mind conjures up all the downright filthy ways I can.

It's a struggle to take my eyes off of us, the vision of my hands on him making it impossible to look away. The emotions between us are palpable, the sexual tension amplifying everything to unimaginable heights. I know he wants to crawl beneath my skin as much as I want to crawl beneath his. We're already impossibly close—skin to skin—and yet somehow it feels like we're still too far apart.

"What do you want me to do to you?" I ask, still kissing him.

"Anything and everything." He raises his arm and hooks it around my neck. "Just need to feel you."

My mouth continues to assault his skin, my gaze watching him melt for me. He's lost in my touch, and every part of me swells with pride at the effect I have on him.

Releasing my grip on his shaft, I bring my hand between us, spreading his cheeks and pressing my hard cock firmly into his crease.

"Fuck," Julian says, his breath labored. "More."

"Bend," I order, placing my hand between his shoulders and pushing him down. Stepping back, I give us both a little bit of room, just enough to allow his body to fold over the bathroom sink. It's spacious enough, but it's surely uncomfortable, and yet he eagerly does what I say; his ass desperate for more.

Reaching for the liquid soap, with one hand, I pump a small amount into my palm. Hissing at the cool temperature on my skin, I rub it up and down my cock before sliding it back between Julian's ass.

I move my hips back and forth, slipping my cock between his cheeks, up and down against his taint, loving the easy, slick glide. Gripping my cock, I line up the tip with his hole and then add the smallest amount of pressure, just enough to make him moan.

Pulling away, I trace his rim with the tip, smearing my pre-cum into his skin. It takes every ounce of control I have not to push inside him and fuck him into oblivion. Hooking an arm around his waist, I bring him back up, flush against me, my cock still nestled between his crease. Wrapping my fingers around his shaft, I stroke him, my hips moving in tandem with my hands.

"Deacon," he pleads.

"What do you want?" I ask again, almost taunting him. "Do you want my lips around you? Your cock sliding in and out of my mouth, hitting the back of my throat?"

Julian's body shudders as an unintelligible whimper echoes around us. "Or do you want my tongue at your hole?"

Heat dances along my spine as my balls tighten at my own words. The plan was to torture him, but we're both very much suffering.

"I'm gonna come," he says in a rush. "Fuck, I'm gonna—"

"Don't even think about it." I drag my hand down to his sac and squeeze it almost painfully. "Not until I'm deep inside you, baby, and you're milking my cock with this beautiful ass of yours."

"Deacon," he cries out, my name both a plea and a demand. "Please."

"Please, what?" I say gently, my hips slowing down, my hand on his cock, now at a standstill. "Stop?"

I teasingly drop my hands to my sides and step away from his body. "Is this what you want?"

Julian's shoulders rise and fall as he tries to regulate his breathing. Turning around, he stands there staring at me, need written all over him. His muscles are tight and strained, his cock bobbing in the air, desperate for attention.

"I'm going to have a shower," he says, repeating the exact words that led us in here in the first place. He glances down at my erection, and his tongue peeks out hungrily. "Want to join me?"

THE SHOWER IS full of steam as I enter it, Julian languidly rubbing soap all over his body as he waits for me. The decision to hang back while he started the shower has my heart rate regulating and my blood pumping slower. It's a constant state of back and forth, wanting the release but wanting the buildup more. We've always been like this, alternating from hard to soft and fast to slow and all the way back again.

Stepping into the spray, I stand behind Julian and let my hands roam over his lathered-up skin as he turns around to face me. Wordlessly, he presses his lips to mine, and our hands keep busy touching and exploring. Mine move down the length of his back, settling on his backside, caressing his firm ass. He pumps the body wash into his hands and lazily washes me.

My tongue dances with his, but it's a slow dance, our mouths moving without urgency. Our bodies continue to meld together, skin against skin, hands everywhere and nowhere all at once. It's the prelude to the main event, the introduction to the night, the beginning of the rest of our lives.

We take turns rinsing one another, my fingers grazing his nipples, his skating my length. I wash his hair and he rinses mine. If my lips aren't on his, his eyes are getting lost in mine, nothing but the purest love between us.

In silence, I turn off the water and watch Julian step out of the shower and dry himself. I reach for a towel, but he swats my arm away and grabs it himself.

"Let me," he says.

He starts at my hair and makes his way down my body—my torso, my groin, my thighs. He lowers himself to his knees, heat-filled eyes glancing up at me expectantly, and suddenly we're back to the hot and heavy portion of the evening.

Extending my arm, I hold it out for him, and he takes it, rising up to his feet. I guide us out of the bathroom, and he leads us toward the bed. I push him onto the mattress and then quickly detour to our bag and grab the lube.

Upon my return, Julian is sitting on the edge of the mattress, stroking himself. I haphazardly throw the bottle on the bed and kneel between his spread legs.

He cards his fingers through my hair as I begin to trail kisses up the inside of his thigh. I bury my face in his groin, breathing him in, the whole day somehow narrowing down to this very moment.

I live for him, and not in a he's-the-only-reason-I'm-alive

way but that everything I do is for him, to make him feel cherished and wanted and loved.

Me on my knees, vowing to love and worship him.

"This…" Despite my arousal, my voice is laced with so much emotion, it almost feels hard to breathe. "This is where I want to start and end every day. With you."

JULIAN

After a day filled with nothing but love, it's overwhelming how much more there is to feel and say. Deacon, on his knees in front of me, somehow still surprising me at every turn.

I love that there are so many layers to him. He's a man of juxtapositions, hard and soft, teacher and student, dominant and submissive, flexible and firm. He truly is whatever I need him to be in *every* moment.

My cock aches at his nearness. I'm torn between the slow build and the eventual release. I love the way both things feel, because there is something so incredibly satisfying about being able to touch and explore and torture and tease all in the same breath. Even after all these years.

Pushing my legs farther apart, Deacon finally puts his mouth where I need it most. Pressing open-mouthed kisses along the length of my cock, he cradles my sac in one hand, wrapping his fingers around my dick with the other.

He guides my shaft between his lips, the wet heat of his mouth all I can feel. Brown eyes meet his blue, and I watch him watch me as he takes me down his throat. My eyes become fixed on the bob of his head and the hollow of his cheeks as he eagerly licks and sucks.

Firm, callused hands grip the back of my thighs, lifting my legs into the air and pushing me back onto the mattress. With my knees to my chest, Deacon grazes his lips down my length and past my taint, the flat of his tongue teasing my hole.

Deacon knows every button to push. Over the years, not only has he spent time and effort becoming familiar with a man's body, but he spent time and effort becoming familiar with *my* body. There isn't any part of me he doesn't know. He knows what sounds I make, and how to make sure I make them.

My back arches off the bed as he spears his tongue in and out of me, feasting on me. He's trying to torture me, and it's working.

The snick of a bottle opening adds to the anticipation, and despite being intimately familiar with the sound, my breath hitches and goosebumps pebble my skin when Deacon replaces his tongue with his cold, lube-covered fingers.

"Fuck," I hiss as he pushes two slick digits inside me.

He effortlessly glides them in and out, scissoring his fingers, making me needier on every stroke. My body writhes when he grazes my prostate, my cock hard, aching, and leaking on my stomach.

"Driving you crazy never gets old." With his fingers still deep inside me, he rises up off his knees and bends at the waist to meet my mouth. "You're so beautiful laid out for me. Desperate for me."

I taste myself on his tongue, and it only makes me hungrier and greedier for more. I devour his mouth as three of his fingers thrust in and out of my hole. He's knuckle deep, stretching me, filling me, but it isn't enough.

"Want my cock?" he taunts.

I clench around him. "Like my next breath."

Deacon drags out his fingers and slaps my ass, the emptiness has an unintelligible sound leaving my mouth. He shuffles us both up the mattress, maneuvering us till he's leaning against the headboard, thighs spread wide and cock resting beautifully against his stomach.

His lust-filled eyes dance over my body as he strokes himself, smearing his pre-cum up and down his length. Searching for the lube, I find the bottle within arm's reach and liberally squeeze some into my palm.

Straddling his thighs, I wrap my hand around him and make a mess of his cock. His large hands reach around to my ass, squeezing and caressing. "Make sure you're ready too."

Our gazes lock as he spreads my cheeks. Still slick, I know this is just for show, and like a good husband, I perform. I run my fingers down my crease and tease my hole, even my own touch too much. I breach myself, one digit and then another, and when Deacon teases my rim, adding to the pressure and the pleasure, I beg, "Please, Deac. Fuck me. Please."

Nudging me forward, my hands land on his shoulders, catching myself. My head falls between us, and I have the perfect view of him lining his beautiful cock up with my ass. His crown presses against my hole, and my head snaps up as we both groan in anticipation.

His hand reaches for my face, his thumb skating across my jaw, the switch from greedy to gentle unmissable.

"Let me watch you fall apart, baby," he says. "I want to see you come on my cock.'

The words are filthy, but his voice is nothing but tender.

I lower myself onto him, inch by inch, the feeling of fullness overwhelming yet welcome. My chest aches with the feeling of coming home, content with the sense of belonging that comes with loving and being loved by this man.

His hand curls around my neck, bringing my mouth to his. The kiss is full of adoration and reverence as he wordlessly hands me control.

In complete sync with one another, I take and he gives, over and over, up and down.

"I love you," he says against my lips, our bodies flush, his cock buried deep. "I love being so wrapped up in you that your heart beats for us and my lungs breathe for us. There is no beginning and no end, there's just you and me."

I want to cry and I want to come, my heart so full it feels like a stretched balloon, my dick so hard it throbs. His hips rock up into me, his cock nudging my prostate, and every part of me feels like it will spill over. I slam my mouth to his as he wraps his hand around my heavy length, unable to formulate the right words, knowing my body will do it justice.

I rise and fall in desperation, riding him, using him, owning him. He wants to start every day with me and I want to end every day with him. The sound of skin slapping skin fills the room as tingles race down my spine and my balls tighten in anticipation. Our bodies move in a heated frenzy. The love between us is palpable, Deacon and I trying to encompass the magnitude of our love in every movement.

Thrust. I love you. *Stroke.* I want forever with you. *Touch.* I would die without you. *Kiss.* I will always choose you.

"Deacon," I cry out. "I'm so close."

"Me too. Come with me," he commands as his hand

pumps my shaft. "I want to see you come all over me while I fill you up."

Between the promise of what's to come and the adrenaline of the day, I welcome the familiar free-falling feeling as my body explodes in euphoria. The orgasm rocks me to my core, and I shout as thick ropes of cum spill onto Deacon's stomach.

"So fucking beautiful," Deacon growls, effortlessly rolling us over till my back is flat against the mattress. My legs are spread wide, my body open for him, as he brutally thrusts into me. I feel his cock pulse and twitch inside me as his climax hits. He moans in my ear as his cum floods my hole.

My chest rises and falls, my body lazy and lax, as we both come down from the high, neither one of us able to speak, neither one of us wanting to move. We stare at one another in contented silence, nothing else in the room besides the smell of sex and the sound of both of us breathing.

Deacon's cock softens and I dread the thought of him leaving my body. As if he can read my mind, his gaze catches on mine, and I gasp as he replaces his shaft with his fingers, pushing his cum deep inside me. It's possessive and primal, and just another way to remind me I'm his and he's mine.

No beginning. No end.

Only him and me.

Me and him.

Husbands.

PART 2
THE LIFE WE CHOSE

JULIAN

Looking down at the baby girl in my arms, I slowly but reluctantly begin to lower her into her crib. Swaddled tightly, she is the epitome of peace, an absolute contrast to the tired, screaming baby she was only minutes ago.

Soft lips press against the back of my neck, and goose-bumps erupt all over my skin as strong arms wrap around my waist. My body relaxes into his as Deacon rests his chin on my shoulder, both of us staring at the little girl who has changed our very existence. From the inside out, every part of us is different now. It's like you lay eyes on your child for the first time and, on autopilot, your mind and heart shift and change to accommodate and you're no longer the man who loves another man unconditionally. You're now the man who loves another man unconditionally *and* will lay your life at the feet of his family to love and adore and protect and to serve.

I remember our first conversation about having our own children, both of us naked, wrapped up in one another on our wedding night, two years ago, the amount of love between us incomparable. My chest felt like it was going to explode, and every touch from Deacon made me feel weightless and invincible.

"Do you want to have kids?" he'd whispered into the night air.

His question conjured up image after image of a life I never even thought to dream of. A life filled with a myriad of love and care and happiness neither of us had grown up with.

I could see it, clear as day—love founded in the depths of despair, made way for a life both of us so desperately wanted.

"We're going to spend the whole night watching her, aren't we?" Deacon says quietly.

I answer with a nod. "I'm afraid so."

Standing there, in silence, I feel the love between us and for her grow, inch by inch with every second that passes. I take in her round face and cherubic cheeks, all red and flustered from her crying. Her lips press together in an adorable pout, and it takes all my strength not to pick her up and cradle her to my chest.

"Come on, baby," Deacon says, walking me backward. "You need to sleep."

After I fuss over the baby monitor and make sure to leave the bedroom door ajar, I find Deacon sitting on the edge of our bed, elbows on his knees, head in his hands.

Walking over, I stand in front of him and nudge his legs apart so I can stand between them. Dropping his hands, he tips his head up to look at me, eyes meeting mine as he places his hands on my hips.

I thread my fingers through the strands of his short hair. "Are you okay?"

He exhales, heavy and loud, but I don't miss the way his

eyes begin to well with unshed tears. "I don't think it ever really hit home, how much they went through till we had her."

My chest feels tight, guilt and sadness sitting heavy on my shoulders. Two years ago, our friends, Jesse and Leo, lost their daughter, and today we were given the privilege of joining them as they commemorate her memory. While having empathy is one thing, imagining it to be your own child is almost paralyzing.

"I don't ever want to know what that feels like," I add.

"I thought with Rhett, we kind of knew what grief looked like, but losing your child..." His voice trails off, and I don't have to be a mind reader to know where his thoughts are headed.

Or how often he's had these thoughts since having Reese.

"Maybe I was—"

I tighten my hold on his hair, pulling his head back, ensuring he's looking at nothing else but me.

"Don't," I say firmly, holding his gaze. "Don't make excuses for her."

He shakes his head, trying to loosen my grip on him, but I don't budge.

"It's not the same thing," I remind him.

"She lost her son," he argues. "I can't imagine—"

I place my hand over his mouth, silencing him. "It's not about Rhett dying, and you know it."

His silence was expected, but still bothers me. It's always where the conversation ends up lately, but the way the text message on my phone felt like it was burning a hole in my pocket, I know we're going to have to talk about her very soon.

For years, it was understood that she was no longer part

of our lives; everyone knew that. Our decision wasn't easy, but there was no denying it needed to happen. Elaine Sutton was not someone who brought anything positive to our lives. It was surreal to connect this version of her to the version of the woman who practically raised me, but it wasn't enough for me to falter when it came to putting Deacon first.

Having Reese has softened us both. Becoming parents is everything you ever imagined, while simultaneously being unlike anything you've ever experienced before.

I have loved blood relatives, I have found family in strangers, but nothing ever compares to something that is only yours. I thought my heart was full with Deacon in my life, but nobody prepared me for my own capacity to love beyond him.

It also made it even harder for me to comprehend how Elaine treated Deacon poorly for so long. Especially when he was finding his feet as a person.

I drop my hand from his mouth. "It's been a long day," I say on a sigh. "And Reese will be up soon."

At three months old, she still wakes up in the middle of the night to feed, and unfortunately all the love in the world can't stamp out the exhaustion from broken sleep.

I hold my hand out to him and patiently wait for him to take it. With a resigned sigh, his palm connects with mine and I pull him up and off the bed and to me.

"I love you," I remind him.

"I love you too." He kisses me softly. "Let's get into bed before I fall asleep standing up."

We try to take turns with night feeding, but we both end up awake, sitting in the dark, staring at one another in awe of this little family we've created.

Despite the endless wave of tiredness, you don't want to miss a single thing.

When deciding on which route to take in order to grow our family, both Deacon and I decided to keep our options open and whatever would be, would be. Between foster courses to make it easier for us to adopt, and researching egg donors, surrogates, and the costs, we covered every angle of every possibility.

It seemed like the stars aligned with our egg donor and our surrogate, and that became the route that would lead us to Reese. A perfect match at every turn, it became an unusually smooth process, all of it feeling very kismet-like. And with Reese in our lives now, I can't imagine a life where she isn't in it.

Both of us dressed in lounge pants and a t-shirt, we brush our teeth and prepare to climb into bed. It's so very domestic, and my favorite thing about us. I love the mundane and the repetitive routine, because somehow, being just ours, it still feels so very fresh and brand new.

"Baby monitor?" Deacon asks as he puts his cell on the charger and slips into his side of the bed.

Like every night, I check it's charging, at the right angle, and the app on my phone can notify either of us of when she wakes up, despite our "do not disturb" status.

"All done," I answer before lying down. "Hopefully tonight is the night she decides she's over the middle of the night feed."

An arm circles my waist and Deacon brings my whole body to his, curling himself around me. He places his lips to the nape of my neck and just breathes me in.

My eyes fall closed as we bask in the silence; the day that was, the day that will be.

"Julian," he whispers.

Wordlessly, I answer him, turning myself in his arms, giving him my full attention. Surprising me, he slams his mouth on mine, and my whole body melts. The kiss feels like an exchange of life and air and a union of want and weariness.

Keeping his lips fixed to mine, I hook my leg over his hip, till we're intertwined in one another. Becoming new parents means we're in a season of our life where the bond is more emotional than physical. Time is of the essence, our energy levels are past depleted, and yet we're both desperate for the connection.

Words are nowhere to be found as his cock thickens against my own. We move like a well-oiled machine, our bodies and minds in sync, kissing, licking, grinding, over and over again.

Our heavy breathing fills the quiet room as desperation fuels us. We're in our own little vortex, this silent understanding of just how much we need one another.

I don't know if it's all the emotion from today, the wild ride of the last three months, or just the constant insatiable ache that exists within me, knowing that every moment we have together in this life would never be enough.

"Pull me out," Deacon says in a hurried breath. "Fuck, baby, I need to feel your hands on me."

My fingers fumble between us, trying to push down the waistband of his pants, and then my own. It's awkward and uncoordinated, and so full of frenzy as we discard the one piece of clothing we both have on and begin rubbing against one another, relishing in the friction.

With my leg back around his hip, I wrap my hand around us both, squeezing and stroking, as our hips rock in tandem, desperately fucking my fist. The glide of his cock against mine is slick and sticky as I smeared pre-cum up all over us.

If there was any finesse in this moment, it's well and truly gone now, our kisses nothing but teeth and tongues, sloppy and messy.

Pulling me closer, Deacon's hand lands on my ass, squeezing and caressing my flesh. When he ghosts a finger over my crease, my body shudders, and there's no way to stop the needy whine that leaves my mouth.

Heat licks at my spine as my balls tighten, my nerve endings on edge, with every inch of contact between us.

"Deac," I manage to breathe out. "I can't. I'm gonna—"

It's a struggle to speak, the tone of my voice a new and yet familiar combination of tiredness and arousal.

Catching me off guard, I feel Deacon press the tips of two fingers against my taint. I cry out when he adds enough external pressure on my prostate, and without any warning, my head snaps back on a groan and I come, spilling between us, all over my hands.

"You're so fucking beautiful when you come," Deacon says hoarsely, his mouth below my ear. One hand slips between us as I come down from my orgasm, stroking his own cock. I try to join in but every part of me feels like Jell-O.

Instead, Deacon grabs my sticky hand and brings my fingers to his mouth, sucking them clean. "I want you in my mouth," I say on a whim. "It's the only part of me that can move right now, and I want to suck on your cock the same way you're sucking on my fingers."

"Sir, yes, sir," Deacon says with a chuckle. "Let me get right on that."

As he maneuvers himself over me, I shift my body up to meet him at the right angle. His legs straddle my upper body as he leans forward to place his hands on the headboard.

"This sight will never get old."

I reach for him, but he swats my hand away. "I thought you were too tired to move. Hands by your side, baby. Lie still and let me fuck your mouth."

DEACON

"Hey."

My eyes fly open at the familiar voice, just in time to catch my friend and coworker, Jesse, kick my feet off a stool in our lunchroom

"You have a home, you know," he says dryly. "With a bed and maybe even a husband and a baby."

"Ha.Ha. Very funny," I say dryly. "I can nap on my lunch break."

"You could nap at home," he reiterates, putting his hands on his hips. "I don't know how many times I have to tell you to go home. You're not needed here."

It's partially true. Duquette's Drives has grown exponentially over the years, into something completely unexpected. When I'd set my sights on working with cars, I'd anticipated doing it for the rest of my life, my body carrying the physical load way past its expiry date.

But Wade and I somehow managed to stumble on the gift that keeps on giving—running a successful garage, and expanding and owning another three more. These days we work less with our hands and more with our heads, dabbling in the occasional restoration work, when the right project comes up.

As we've both started families, it's the perfect situation to be in—spending more time doing the things we enjoy and spending less time hustling to chase our tails. So, I understand why Jesse is questioning my presence. But some days I just can't leave this place alone.

The smell of oil and gasoline calms me in a way I can't explain. The routine and the familiarity grounding me, especially when I have something on my mind.

And I definitely have something on my mind.

"So," Jesse drawls. "Why are you here?"

Sighing, I lower my legs and sit upright, running a hand over my tired face. "Can I ask you something?"

A crease forms on Jesse's forehead as he pulls up a chair beside me. "Is everything okay?"

It isn't every day I ask my friends for advice, but it also isn't every day I feel so off-kilter. There's nothing wrong, per se, but my thoughts have been straying to my mother a lot, and that hasn't happened in years. It makes me antsy and uncertain, but ever since we had Reese, she's always there at the back of my mind.

"Everything is more than okay," I answer truthfully. "Just always surprised by how much having kids changes a person."

Jesse blows out a long breath of air. "You think you know, but it's like suddenly there's two versions of you, before them and after them."

While Jesse and his husband Leo lost their baby girl, they're also parents to an amazing sixteen-year-old, Raine. So, if there's anyone who is more than qualified to walk me through my thoughts, it's him.

"I keep thinking about my mom," I confess. "I look at Reese and I think of my mother, and I just wonder if she felt all the same things when she had me."

Glancing down at my feet, I purposely avoid meeting Jesse's gaze. Even though it's my choice to open this can of worms, vulnerability is not something I enjoy feeling. It's half the reason I haven't spoken to Julian or Wade, because they know me too well, and it wouldn't just be a conversation taken at face value. It would be an inquisition where they'd both manage to crack my chest open to see what's inside, and I'm not ready to go there yet.

"It's stupid," I say quickly. "Don't even worry about it."

Before I have the chance to stand up and walk away, Jesse's hand lands on my shoulder. "If you want to talk to your mother, talk to her."

And that's the crux of it. I don't really know if I want to talk to her or if the birth of my daughter is making me feel nostalgic for something that more than likely never existed.

When the silence lingers between us, Jesse makes the whole thing even more complicated by asking, "Have you spoken about this with Julian?"

I shake my head. "I don't want to bother him with it."

"Deacon," he says seriously. "Speaking from experience, that's not how marriage works. Trust me, he wants you to bother him with it."

Jesse is a hundred percent right, but I need to work out how to broach the subject of her with him, without shutting down. I know it isn't warranted, but I feel shame for even thinking about her. Almost like I'm not allowed to change my mind or question decisions past me made.

"Seriously." Jesse squeezes my shoulder as he rises up off his chair. "Go home and talk to him."

As Jesse leaves the break room, my phone vibrates, and I know without a doubt it'll be Julian.

Glancing down at the screen, I take in the photo he's sent through of Reese awake and comfortably lying on his chest. Then I read the text underneath.

We're missing you.

My fingers dance across the screen.

Not for too much longer. Be home soon.

Turning the key, I push open our front door and try not to make too much noise. Chances are Reese is already awake, but if she is asleep, I'll do anything necessary to ensure she stays asleep.

Toeing off my shoes, I walk through the house, noting the soft hum of a tune coming from Julian before laying eyes on him in the kitchen. Julian's got Reese across his chest in the baby carrier while he lines up her bottles, filling them with water and formula.

He looks so natural preparing her food for the night, and it's hard to imagine a life where he didn't know how to be the most perfect father to our daughter. When our embryo had been successfully transferred, we'd sat down and discussed all the ways our lives would change and which changes would suit us best. Anticipating things we had heard about from friends, or things we'd read in books.

We're blessed in ways I never anticipated, and the ability to be home with our daughter in her first few months of life is one of them.

It's no surprise that, as a high school teacher, Julian is adored by both the faculty and the students. His boss has worked hard to allow Julian three months of paternity leave and the option to return part-time. The deadline of that decision is coming up quickly, but I know it isn't something Julian wants to discuss yet.

He's basking in parenthood, and I have no desire to have him prioritize anything else.

And as Jesse so eloquently pointed out, I have free rein now. I don't need to be tied down to a garage and under cars twelve hours a day. It's the time in my life that I get to enjoy the fruits of my labor.

And coming home to them is exactly what that is.

Coming up behind Julian, I curl my hand around his waist and kiss the back of his neck. As if he sensed my arrival, he turns around with a welcoming smile. With Reese between us, I lower my head to kiss the top of hers.

"How are my two favorite people?" I ask him, my voice low and soft.

"Happy you're home," he whispers back. "I'm about to make us lunch."

"Why don't you finish this"—I point to the bottles—"and I'll make us lunch."

Julian glances down at Reese. "Should I try moving her to the crib?"

There's every chance she'll wake up, and if I know Julian as well as I think I do, he's going to change his mind in less than three seconds and keep her sleeping on his chest.

"She'll wake up anyway," he says, confirming my thoughts. "I may as well keep her on me so she'll sleep longer."

We aren't the type of parents who give too much mind

to how our baby sleeps or where. For the most part, there's a routine centered around when Reese sleeps, but where she sleeps is wherever works in that moment for both her and us. And truth be told, sometimes you want to hold your daughter close and get lost in that new baby scent as she sleeps across your chest.

The thing about being a parent and forever grieving a sibling is, the loss feels tangible in a way I would've never understood without Reese. It's a crippling realization to know that, for any reason, life could exist without her. It cuts just as deeply living and knowing every minute that passes, is a minute we would never get back. Some days, routine and good habits feel trivial. If we want to hold her in our arms while she sleeps instead of putting her in her crib, then so be it.

"Lie down on the couch with her if you want. Have a nap, and we can eat when you wake up," I suggest. "Or we can eat now and then you can sleep."

"Lunch," he answers. "One thing at a time; she might not even last that long."

I chuckle softly. "Fair enough. Do you want leftovers or a turkey sub?"

"A sub sounds good," he says through a yawn.

I point in the direction of our living room. "Couch now. I'll be out with your food soon."

"I love you," he says, his voice nothing more than a tired sigh. "If I'm asleep by the time you come out, please wake me up because I'm hungry."

Laughing, I turn away and focus on making lunch and ignoring his request. If he's asleep when I'm done, there's no way I'll be waking him up, and we both know it.

Grateful that I opened up to Jesse, I grab everything I

need for our sandwiches, and bask in the mundane task of making lunch for my husband while our daughter sleeps. Just as I load each one onto a plate, the sound of something vibrating against the counter catches me off guard. Looking around the kitchen, I spot Julian's cell by the tin of formula, and notice the lit-up screen.

Quickly, I grab the phone and slip it in my pocket before picking up the plates and walking them to Julian. Placing them down on the coffee table, I'm surprised to see Julian awake with the television on, the volume muted.

"I was sure you'd be asleep," I tell him.

"You're home," he says while stroking Reese's back. He's undone the carrier enough that it's still on his body, but she's no longer covered by it. "I want to hear about your morning at work."

Unable to help myself, I bend over and kiss him on the forehead.

"I shouldn't have gone," I admit, lowering myself to the floor beside him, between the couch and the coffee table. "I needed to clear my head, and I went there instead of talking to you."

Julian's brows knit together, my admission catching him off guard. "What's wrong?"

"Nothing." Before I can reach for our lunch, my pocket vibrates again, reminding me I have his phone.

"Oh," I add nonchalantly. "This was making some noise in the kitchen. Seems like someone really wants to talk to you."

I awkwardly raise my hip up off the floor and shove my hand into my front pocket. Dragging it out, it's unavoidable to see the name sliding across the top of the screen.

I can feel my face scrunch up in confusion as my gaze

darts between the screen and Julian, who is looking at me with an expression that undoubtedly matches mine. It's unexpected and yet somehow a coincidence, but one thing I know for sure is seeing my mother's name on the screen is definitely unwelcome.

JULIAN

With my cell in Deacon's hand, and the look of shock turning into complete mortification, I know exactly who's name is on the screen. The incessant buzz is the only sound between us as he looks at me expectantly, wanting and deserving an explanation.

"She's been texting me," I reveal, my voice gentle as I deliver the news. I reach for the phone, decline the call, and switch off my phone, just to ensure we're not interrupted.

His gaze drifts to Reese before landing back on me, somehow keenly aware of the reasons his mother has now chosen to reach out.

"Come here." Slowly, I sit up, careful not to wake Reese, knowing it's inevitable at this point, and make room for him beside me. It takes a minute for him to rejoin the conversation, his mind derailing, his thoughts floating to somewhere I'm not. As he finally settles next to me, I hand him our daughter, who curls up perfectly against his chest, knowing she'll be the calm to his storm.

"I should've told you." A hand lands on my thigh, silencing me. I know I haven't done anything wrong, but his touch and close proximity are a relief all the same. I thread my fingers through his as he sinks into the couch, tips his head back, and closes his eyes.

"I've been thinking about her all day today," he eventually confesses. "Thinking, maybe I do want to speak to her now that we have Reese..." His voice trails off, replaced with a deep inhale and a loud exhale before continuing. "But when I saw her name on the screen, *everything* came rushing back."

"We don't owe her anything," I remind him. "*You* don't owe her anything."

He tips his head to the side, finally looking at me, his blue eyes looking sad and desolate in a way I haven't seen in years.

"Have you spoken to her?" he asks.

Reese predictably starts to wriggle in his hold before I can answer, and I have to wonder how much of this Band-Aid we can rip off all at once, or is it determined to be the wound that keeps on bleeding.

"I haven't spoken to her," I tell him truthfully. "She's texted. More than once," I inform. "If she's calling, I'm assuming she's getting sick and tired of waiting for me to respond."

"She wants to meet Reese, doesn't she?"

My teeth tug at the skin of my lips as I nod, my anxiety over all of this finally rising up to the surface.

"Why didn't you tell me?"

The question is valid, but I'm certain he isn't going to appreciate my answer. "Because I didn't want to," I say too bluntly. "Hasn't she ruined enough?"

"So what I want for Reese doesn't matter?"

"That's not at all what this is, and you know it." My voice is low but stern as I continue. "But this is exactly my point. There's nothing about the mere mention of her that doesn't bring you anguish, and I think it's okay for me not to want that for you and our daughter."

"You still should've told me," he says, his jaw clenched.

I know he's right, but my instinct to protect our family only has me seeing red. I know there is a middle ground, I know there is a space for us to talk about this rationally, but I'm not the same person I was the last time we spoke to Elaine. I'm not the same person I was when we got married. I am both of those men and so much more.

I'm full, with more love and more loyalty, and there is no way this woman is getting to them without going through me. If that means fighting with Deacon to protect them both, then I'll do it. In every lifetime they will come first, and I know despite his confusion and anger, he knows that.

He knows *me*.

A small, melodic sounding whine leaves Reese's mouth, interrupting us and effectively putting our conversation on pause.

"I'll get her a bottle," I tell Deacon as I rise up off the couch.

With the bottle already prepared and in the fridge, it only takes me a few minutes to heat it up and check the temperature on the inside of my wrist. When it's ready for Reese to eat, I stride back into the living room, the sight of Deacon smiling playfully at our daughter as he changes her diaper, stopping me in my tracks.

This is what I want to keep, selfish or not. I want to live in this bubble with him and her and have nothing else taint that. My eyes land on the uneaten sandwiches, and I tell myself this can wait.

Elaine Sutton can fucking wait.

Handing Deacon the bottle, I gesture to our food. "Can

we at least eat lunch first and finish this conversation later? I don't want it to go to waste."

Seeming a little bit calmer, he nods, and I take it as my cue to head back into the kitchen and grab us both a soda. Sitting side by side, I eat my sandwich first while he feeds Reese. Besides her cute little suckling sounds, we sit in complete silence. It's not awkward or tense, but it's that moment of quiet that speaks the loudest. Our anger and hostility isn't at one another, it's at finding ourselves in another impossible situation, all these years later, at the hands of Deacon's mother.

It takes about the same time for me to finish my sub as it does for Reese to finish her bottle.

"Let me burp her," I offer. "And you can eat."

When he hands me Reese, I put her over my shoulder and begin rubbing circles in the center of her back while Deacon takes his turn to have lunch. Just as we settle back into the silence, a loud belch breaks through the invisible, mesh-like wall between us, making us lock eyes and laugh.

"Are we okay?"

Reaching for me, he skates his fingers down the length of my jaw.

"I love you," he says, and the anxiety in my chest loosens ever so slightly. "We're always going to be okay," he assures me. "Nobody gets to rock our boat. Nobody gets to have that power over us."

Especially not her.

Leaning into his touch, I hear what he doesn't say, and wholeheartedly agree. "I should've told you about it," I admit. "I just don't know what this means for us, and I was scared."

When Deacon remains silent, I push and try to bring up

something he said earlier. "You mentioned wanting to speak to her again. Does that still stand?"

Blowing out a long breath, he bends over and places his empty plate on the coffee table. He delays the conversation by reaching for his soda, and I watch him take small sips and stare into the empty space directly in front of him.

Giving him the time he so obviously needs, I mosey through the usual steps after a feed, checking Reese's diaper and then putting her down on her play mat. Instead of sitting beside her and reading to her or playing with her, I decide that she'll be okay while I wait for Deacon to tell me what's going on in that head of his.

"Daddy will be back," I say to Reese as I kiss her on the forehead.

Content with the way she's waving her arms and her legs, I head back over to Deacon and try to get to the bottom of what we're both feeling. Squeezing between the table and the couch, I kneel in front of him and intertwine my fingers with his. I bring them to my lips, kissing each of his knuckles. "Talk to me."

For the first time since he saw his mother's name on my cell phone screen, it feels like the fog hanging over him might have finally lifted.

"Tell me," I urge. "Where do we go from here?"

I catch him glancing at Reese before darting his gaze back to mine, that paternal instinct now ingrained in every moment.

"I think of how much I love her." He pauses, his throat bobbing, and I watch the struggle of what he wants to say next play out on his face. "And how much it would *kill* me if I existed in a world where she did not.

"And I have to give credit where credit is due, because how my mother lived through it is beyond me. But..." He closes his eyes and shakes his head vehemently, almost like he's trying to rid himself of something. "But then I think of how much I love that little girl and how I would rather die than make her feel a sliver of the way my mother made me feel."

Despite the fury racing through my veins, there is a bruised, tender part of my heart that throbs and aches whenever I think of our past and everything Deacon and I had endured, separately and together, and right now every ounce of pain it feels is for him.

"And I want what she has with Vic's kids," he confesses. "Otherwise, it's just one more thing I miss out on. Something Reese misses out on."

Even though the distance between us is minimal, I climb up onto the couch and straddle him, cradling his face in my hands.

"Whatever you want, we'll do," I tell him, despite every molecule in my body opposing contact with her. I could acknowledge that this is a decision Deacon needs to make, with no input from me. I can't give him my opinion or sway him. In good times and bad, when it's hard and easy, this is the exact moment marriages are made of.

"When she calls you next," he says, tears spilling from his eyes and landing on my hands, "tell her if she has any hope of meeting Reese, she needs to talk to me first."

DEACON

Anticipating the alarm on my cell to go off soon, I reach for the phone and quickly switch it off. After waking up for a third time, I gave up on trying to sleep and have been lying here, staring at the ceiling ever since.

Just like I asked, Julian waited for the next time my mother reached out, and passed on my message. The only issue was I didn't think she would call the very next day, and I didn't expect to have her flying to Seattle the week after that.

We agreed to meet here, with my father and Julian. Victoria was flying in with Mom and she would pick Reese up from Wade and Christie's. It isn't ideal, and I know Julian is torn between being there for both of us, but I refuse to risk my mother accidentally meeting Reese. It's a hard limit, and I love and know him well enough that whether he's with me or with Reese, our family is his priority.

It feels like an over-the-top secret mission, but protecting our peace is important, and in case this blows up in my face, I need to make sure this meeting does as little damage as possible.

My anxiety is borderline unmanageable, the lack of sleep proof of that. I can't decide what I want. Do I just really want to lay eyes on the only woman to ever break my heart?

The sound of Julian's phone vibrating interrupts my thoughts and has my anxiety increasing tenfold. It's six o'clock on a Friday morning.

Who the hell would be calling now?

When the vibration continues and Julian doesn't flinch, I stretch my body over his and grab it. I catch a glimpse of an unfamiliar number before it stops.

"Fuck," I mutter. "Juli—"

Vibration from my phone cuts me off, and now my mind is whirling at who it could be. I launch myself off of Julian and dive for my cell. Noticing the same number, I quickly swipe at my screen and answer.

"Hello."

"Hello." A woman's voice comes through the phone. "Is this Deacon Sutton?"

"Speaking."

I feel Julian sitting up behind me, his bare skin grazing mine.

"Hello," she repeats, her tone a little less formal. "I'm so sorry to call this early, my name is Gwen from Family Services."

At her introduction, I put the phone on speaker and turn to face Julian, our eyes locked, my heart racing.

"We have you and your husband listed as foster parents," she says, and Julian's head bobs up and down before the rest of the sentence even leaves her mouth. "Our database says your status is available," she continues. "And there is a young boy; he's four and a half. His parents passed away in a car accident and he's currently recovering from minor injuries at Seattle Presbyterian," she explains. "He has a grandmother in a nursing home and no other living relatives."

I quickly catch the tear that threatens to fall down Julian's cheek, knowing exactly what he's thinking, knowing exactly what this reminds him of.

"He'll be staying in the hospital over the weekend," she says. "But we wanted to touch base and see if you and your husband have the capabilities to take him in."

My mind drifts back to everything we've been through up until this point, the decision to make ourselves available to be parents in whatever way that looked like. But all of that was before Reese, all of that was before a little, beautiful baby girl buried herself into our hearts and lives and became our *only* priority.

"We have a daughter now," I inform her. "A three-month-old."

"Okay," she drawls. "There isn't really much tim—"

"We're not saying no," I reassure her, and Julian, whose face has fallen. "We just need a minute to see what that would look like for us now."

I talk to both of them, because while I know my husband has a bleeding heart, we have to take the time and make this decision based on facts and not on emotions.

"Please," I say earnestly. "Can you give us the weekend?"

I know it's a long shot, but I have enough experience to know what will be, will be. Because I married my dead brother's boyfriend, and nothing screams *against all odds* more than the improbability of our union. If we were supposed to have this child in our lives, one way or another it would happen, and I genuinely believe that.

"I can," she says. "But I also do have to check with other families to keep his options open. We can't put all our eggs in one basket and come Monday morning you say no and we're back at square one."

The words aren't harsh but a reality. Her tone is no nonsense, evidence that the little boy is her priority and she's going to do everything in her power to make sure he has somewhere soft to land when he leaves that hospital.

I like that. And if we can't be what he needs, then at least he has her.

"Okay, we'll call you back either way."

"Hopefully I'll be talking to you soon," Gwen says politely before hanging up.

I stare at the cell as the call disconnects, nothing but silence left behind. My mind nothing but a jumbled mess, filled with dread and dreams and happy ever afters that may or may not be within everyone's reach.

Finally, I raise my head and am met with Julian's sad eyes.

"Please don't look at me like that," I say. "We have a lot going on right now."

He lets his body fall back to the mattress, sighing. "You can be right and I can still be sad, both of those things can exist."

Sliding back beneath the blankets beside him, I pull him into my arms, his head resting on my chest. "We're only just getting used to having a baby in our lives," I say. "How would we even juggle two?"

I hate playing bad cop, but every now and then I have to be the voice of reason. Julian is the ever-present optimist in our relationship, and most of the time it's exactly what we need. What *I* need.

"I don't have the answers," he says. "But filling our house with children doesn't feel like a bad idea. It would be like any other unexpected pregnancy. They're still loved."

I press my mouth to the crown of his head. "I do want what you want. There are just so many variables and so many ways I can fuck it up."

Julian lifts his head, his chin now resting on my chest, his gaze meeting mine. "Firstly, it wouldn't be only you who could fuck it up, it would be both of us. We make the decisions together, which means the consequences are ours, together."

"I don't want to get it wrong," I admit. "Not something like this."

Shuffling up my torso, Julian lays his body on top of mine, propping himself up with his forearms. "Let's put a pin in this," he suggests. "Have a shower. I'll make you breakfast, and after today we can get back to the drawing board and call Gwen on Monday with our answer."

THE SOUND of our doorbell ringing makes me want to puke almost immediately. Everything seemed like a good idea, when it was just that: an idea. But now, my mother is on the other side of a door she has never been welcome to walk through, and I'm hit with a reminder of me, standing outside my childhood home, equally eager and anxious to tell my mother about Julian and me.

Is that how she feels now?

I feel Julian's hand land on my shoulder. "Do you want me to open it? Do you want me to leave you here alone?

Take your Dad into the kitchen? Should we have thought of a safe word?"

An unexpected laugh bubbles out of my mouth, the tension from my shoulders evaporating almost immediately, the slight smirk on Julian's face telling me his verbal faux pas was not at all accidental.

"It'll be fine," I reassure us both. "You know me well enough to know when I've reached my limit."

I know with my whole entire being that Julian wouldn't wait for a safe word. If he sees me in distress, he'll save me, whether I ask for it or not.

Kissing him on the cheek, I take a few steps, closing the distance between me and my parents. Opening the door, I brace myself for an onslaught of emotions that surprisingly never come. I feel almost numb inside as I take in the woman before me.

There is no denying she's aged, from the salt and pepper roots of her short bob to the lines around her eyes and the sides of her mouth. She's smaller somehow, almost like my decision to rid myself of the power she had over me made her somehow less intimidating.

"Deacon," she greets.

If I expected a smile, or some sort of warm, nostalgic meeting, I'm immediately corrected. She's as rigid and defensive as she's ever been, and for some reason this eases my nerves.

I know this version of my mother.

I'm prepared to deal with this version of her.

"Mom." I shift my gaze to the spot beside her, my face softening. "Dad. Come in. How are you?"

"Good," he responds, leaning in for a hug, his voice as gruff as always. My arms circle his body, grateful to have always had his support.

"Thank you for coming," I say softly, and he squeezes me tighter.

"Julian." My mother's voice catches my attention. "It's good to see you."

I can almost hear my own heart sigh at the difference between the two greetings, but I try to move past it and give her the benefit of the doubt. She and I have a history that she and Julian do not.

"Elaine," he says, his voice flat and void of emotion. "Let's sit down."

He guides us into the living room.

Instead of following, my dad wordlessly walks into the kitchen, probably to give us some space and spare us an audience. I don't doubt how hard this is on him, and I'm certain keeping some distance allows him to remain neutral and not influence my decision of whether or not to forgive my mother.

He's shown me time and time again that he's here for me, with or without her, loving me unconditionally like every parent should.

Our living area is big enough that my mother and I don't have to sit too close, but it also means we're in the direct line of sight of each other, and there is no hiding in this moment, for either of us.

My hands are clenched into fists on my knees, my chest filled with so much tense air, it hurts to breathe, but I rip that Band-Aid off anyway.

"What is it that you want, Mom?" Julian's hand covers mine, and I don't miss the way her eyes settle on the subtle, albeit still public display of affection between us.

If it bothers her, she doesn't show it, and if she's happy for us, she doesn't show that either.

"Elaine," Julian says, the tone of his voice undeniably impatient. "You texted for months."

"I know, I know," she rushes out, her gaze darting between us. "I didn't think you would agree, and now I'm here." She shrugs, her lips pursed together. "I realize I didn't really make a plan of what comes next. You have a beautiful home," she compliments. "A good size for a family."

Her words aren't a question, but they're enough for us to segue into why she's really here. But instead of making it easier for her, I sit in silence. If she wants access to her grandchild, she's going to have to work for it.

Her knee begins to bounce, and I steer my thoughts away from the default, from the inherent need and habit to make excuses for her discomfort and wrongdoings.

"Congratulations on starting a family," she eventually says, this time her gaze locked on mine. Her defenses have finally fallen, the smile on her face sad yet hopeful. "Your father says your daughter is beautiful."

DEACON

I n normal circumstances her words would be the perfect introduction for me to beam with pride about how amazing and gorgeous Reese is and just how lucky and grateful we are.

And yet, here I sit, words stiff and stuck in my throat. I'm wondering why exactly I agreed to this, and I'm pissed off nostalgia got the better of me.

"She is," Julian eventually says on our behalf. "We are so lucky to have her in our lives."

"Is she an easy bab—"

"Mom," I say through clenched teeth, my anger surprising all of us. "This wasn't an invitation for small talk."

"Well, I don't know what you want me to say here, Deacon," she says, a little bit exasperated.

"Sorry," I practically shout, my body filled with too much ire to remain seated. "Surely, you didn't come all this way, after all these years, to *not* apologize."

"Of course. I want to put this all behind us."

Shaking my head, I put a hand up to silence her, and

feel Julian rise up off the seat, standing beside me. The blood swimming in my veins is beyond boiling, the heat almost paralyzing. I dig my teeth into my bottom lip, pressing hard, and close my eyes; inhaling and exhaling, desperate for some semblance of calm.

"Mom," I say, blowing out a long, resigned breath. "Say. Sorry."

Opening my eyes, I catch my father's figure brush past my peripheral vision. I expect him to continue walking into my line of sight and stand next to my mother, but it doesn't happen. He just stands there on the sidelines, his attention on his wife, waiting for her to say something.

Waiting for her to say the right thing.

The room is silent and the air thick, each one of us now standing around the living room. Julian places his hand between my shoulder blades, and I give myself the desperately needed reprieve and glance over my shoulder to look at him.

The love and devotion between us, even unspoken, is apparent and obvious, and the perfect epiphany as to why I'm standing here before her. My feelings and thoughts may have been confused and influenced by the softness of raising such a beautiful, innocent baby, but this is not a reunion.

I don't want to make amends or play happy families. I don't want to see what the future holds and make up for everything we've lost.

This moment is the antithesis of "time heals everything."

Not with her and not ever.

This is her chance to give us the apology we deserve. The apology *I* deserve.

It's been years, and it is overdue. And the truth is, I'm

certain it won't even make a difference—but what I do know is I need to hear it.

I hold my hand out to Julian, who steps forward to stand beside me and takes it.

We stand there as a united front as years of pent up anger, disappointment, and heartache just tumble out of my mouth.

"You know what being a father has taught me?" I ask rhetorically. "Actually, do you know what being both a husband and a father has taught me?"

I don't miss the way my mother's eyes widen in surprise as she takes me in. The son she left behind was meek and quiet and amiable to her at all times. The son in front of her no longer lives to placate her feelings.

"Unconditional love," I tell her. "Being a husband and a father has taught me that I love the people in my life unconditionally. Your love has always been conditional." My voice cracks on that last word, and I let it, because I am no longer ashamed of the pain and hurt she caused me. "Your love was like one of those mood rings Victoria used to wear; a different version of it for every version of you.

"As a father, my heart is broken even imagining what it would be like burying a child, and I will never, ever, try to take your grief away from you."

Tears stream down her face, and there is no doubt in my mind they're for Rhett and not for me. "But I was a child. I am *your* child," I say forcefully. "And yet you made me feel like a nuisance, like a bother, like I would be better if I reached all your goalposts, only for you to move every single one when it suited you. I wore the consequences for actions that weren't mine."

"Deacon," she says, her voice shaking. "When Rhett got sick and died, life was—"

"No," I shout, cutting her off. "Stop using him as an excuse. Of course your burden was heavier and harder than most, but what about when he wasn't sick?" I ask.

She furrows her brows at me, and I forge ahead. "Being a father has taught me that I would go to the ends of the earth for my child. But you couldn't do that for me. Everything was too hard or I was too difficult. Or maybe..." I throw my hands up in the air. "Maybe there's just something about me that you don't like."

"Deacon." She steps closer, and despite there still being a significantly decent amount of distance between us, I step backward, not needing the distraction of her proximity to derail the point I'm trying to get across. "How can you say that I don't like my own son? I love you, Deacon."

The three words are like squeezing lemons on fresh cuts, the sting palpable.

"Then why did I feel anything but loved?" The unanswered question hangs between us, but I can't seem to stop the words from leaving my mouth. "You made me feel second-best every chance you got.

"You made me feel second-best in my own relationship." Turning my head, Julian meets my gaze as I confess the worst parts of myself. "You will never ever know what that did to me. You'll never know how close I was to giving up the best thing in my life because of you."

Julian squeezes my hand, shaking his head, his eyes filling with unshed tears. "You will never know how inadequate I have felt, loving this man, because of you."

Finally shifting my gaze away from Julian, I look over to find my mother staring at us and openly sobbing. I should feel some type of way, knowing I've upset her and that she's so distressed, but instead I feel nothing but pity for her. Pity that we're all standing here in this room, strangers to one another, because of her.

"Deacon." She hiccups, and this time I let her talk. "I have plenty of excuses for why I was the way I was, and why I said and did the things I said and did. But I understand that they'll only ever be excuses."

"Can I ask you something?" I say, interrupting her and surprising us both, the thought hitting me like a freight train.

She nods while dabbing at the corner of her eyes with a tissue.

"Why now?"

Confusion is etched on her features. "What do you mean?"

"Why did you reach out now?" I ask. "I had a whole wedding that you didn't seem very adamant on attending."

The silence stretches between us, and I have my second epiphany of the day. A humorless laugh leaves my mouth as my gaze darts between all of us in the room before landing back on her.

"You still can't accept he's mine, can you?"

Her spine stiffens, and it's all the admission I need. Shaking my head, I release my hold on Julian's hand and stride into the kitchen. I absentmindedly grab a clean glass off the dish rack and fill it with water, drinking it all at once.

"Deacon." My mother's voice has my jaw clenching in annoyance, but I bite my tongue, put the empty cup into the sink, and turn around to face her. "I'm trying to explain myself and you're not giving me a chance."

"You're right." Resigned, I cross my arms over my chest. "Please. Explain."

"I am always looking for Rhett," she says. "In a book, in

a song, heck, sometimes I'm even looking for a sign in the middle of Costco. And yes, when I see Julian, I see Rhett.

"I know that the more time I see you two together, in love and doting on your family, the more your relationship will make sense to me."

I huff. Her answer makes sense on paper, but I hate it all the same. "Tell me, Mom. Are you sorry?"

Reaching for me, she places her hand on my forearm, her eyes purposefully locked on mine. "More than you'll ever know."

JULIAN

While Deacon and his mother deserved privacy, Bill and I clearly weren't comfortable or confident in giving it to them. My eyes zero in on Deacon's body language, while the quiet house makes their exchange easy enough to hear.

He looks resigned and defeated, and I have to wonder if her apology is truly just a little too late after all. I hadn't been expecting much, but I think we were both expecting a little bit more than what she's giving.

Time has changed her, and yet there are things about her that are exactly the same, and that includes her inability to be vulnerable for Deacon's sake. She's still too defensive and argumentative, and what he needed was the apology first and everything else to come second.

Instead, that man sliced his chest open and bled on the floor for all of us to see, and she doesn't possess the skills to clean up the mess.

Deacon's eyes dart away from his mother, finally noticing me and Bill for the first time. Straightening his spine, he tips his head to the side, gesturing for me to stand beside him. And I do. With both pride and purpose.

Elaine steps back as I move in closer, and Deacon extends his hand, closing the small gap between us, almost like the smallest distance between us is unbearable. I don't bother paying her any mind, my husband being my priority.

He pulls me into him and presses a kiss against my temple.

"Want to go for a drive?" he whispers into my ear.

Catching me off guard, I turn to face him. "Now?"

"Let's leave them here," he says, referring to his mom and dad. "I need a minute or two. Just you and me."

Deacon isn't usually the spontaneous type, so his request for alone time feels more like a cry for help than a rendezvous. I don't have an objection to Elaine being in our space, because I trust Bill implicitly, and Deacon's needs are always going to be what's most important to me.

When I think about just how much we're dealing with today, it's to be expected that a conversation about the future would be on the horizon. We have a lot to talk about. We have a lot to think about, and right now, between the family and the drama and all the expectations, our house has become unintentionally suffocating.

Glancing over to Bill, I notice him watching us, clearly eavesdropping on our conversation. He gives me a subtle nod, and I take it as our cue to leave.

"Come on." I tug on Deacon's hand. "Let's get out of here."

"I DON'T REMEMBER the last time I ate a burger this good." Deacon groans as he takes the next bite, and I feel the edges of my mouth tip up in a smile. In this moment he looks young and relaxed and so free of the hurt that was in his every expression earlier today. "I also don't remember what it's like to eat a meal without sharing baby duties."

"Mhmm," I agree, shoving a handful of french fries in my mouth. "We took those child-free date nights for granted."

We're at a hole in the wall diner that had been recommended to me by some of my colleagues at work. It's nothing more than a room with a few tables pushed together and a kitchen out back. But the food is mouth-wateringly good.

"We should try and get into a habit of scheduling them more, maybe have Christy and Wade babysit," Deacon muses before quickly shaking his head. "That's a terrible idea. I don't want to have dinner without Reese."

His answer has me chuckling into my food. He's rambling about nothing in particular and everything all at the same time. And it would be unobservant of me to not notice that this is extremely unusual for him. I don't want to pressure or probe him into delving into his feelings, but I can also see that his decision to avoid the tougher conversations isn't sustainable either.

I want him to talk when he's ready, but I also need him to be okay. And there's a fine line between both those things.

Grabbing his cell off the table, he swipes at the screen a few times before bringing it up to his ear.

"Do you think Dad will have left with Mom by the time we get back?" he asks nonchalantly. "Because I'd really love to pick up Reese and take her home."

It's a simple question, but I don't miss the words he's not saying. *I don't want my mother to meet our daughter.*

"Who are you calling?" I ask, quickly putting another fry in my mouth.

"Vic," he replies. "I want to pick up Reese."

Making an executive decision, I lean over the diner table and take the cell out of his hand just as the call connects.

"Hello," Victoria answers

"Hey," I greet, my eyes meeting Deacon's confused ones. "How's Reese?"

"She's good," she coos, her voice taking on that baby-talk tone people do when they're talking to the kid, about the kid. "She just woke up from her nap. How are things over there?"

"They're good," I say, not wanting to give too much away. "We just wanted to let you know it'll be a little bit longer before we come and pick her up."

"Of course. Take your time," she says. "You know she's safe here. Christy and Wade's kids are so obsessed, I don't think they're ready to say goodbye anyway."

"Perfect," I chirp. "We'll call you soon."

Ending the call, I hand an unimpressed Deacon back his phone.

"What was that?" he asks. "I wanted to pick up Reese."

"Baby," I say gently, reaching over the table to place my hand over his. "You know it can be impossible to talk to one another while we're fussing over her."

Dragging his hand out from under mine, he leans back in the chair, almost like he's moving away from me. If I didn't know him well enough, I would take it personally and assume he needs space. And he does need the space, but it isn't from me.

"Tell me," I prompt. "Nothing has changed. Whatever you say, we do."

"But everything has changed," he admits. "*She's* changed. *We've* changed. It went exactly and nothing like how I anticipated it to go."

Our waitress chooses this moment to clear our table. "Can I get you the bill?" she asks while stacking plates on her forearm.

"Yeah, that'll be great, thanks," Deacon answers.

Subconsciously, we pause the conversation, and I wait till the bill is squared away and we're both standing on the sidewalk next to our parked car to continue it. "Do you at least feel better?"

He leans against the car, leg bent at the knee, hands buried deep in the pockets of his jeans. The unseasonably warm weather has him in a white tee, stretched across his broad chest, muscled biceps on full display. He looks exactly like that man I saw standing at the cemetery all those years ago, but his shoulders are less hunched, his expression no longer guarded and harsh.

Right now, more than ever, he looks at peace.

"I feel lighter," he eventually admits, confirming my thoughts. "It feels good to no longer have that sitting on my shoulders. I know we've always spoken about it, and it came up in therapy all those years ago, but it feels good to offload it all to the person who needed to hear it the most."

Moving toward him, he straightens his stance and opens up his arms for me to step into. Placing my hands on either side of his neck, I let my thumb draw circles over his fluttering pulse.

"Do you forgive her?"

I feel his chest rise and fall against my own as he contemplates his answer. "I think I've come to the realization that it was never about forgiving her," he explains. "I wanted her to know more than I wanted to forgive her. I wanted her to know, out of the horse's mouth, just how much damage she's done. And now she does." He shrugs. "And forgiving her doesn't change anything. I don't think we can ever go back. Or forward. At least not Mom and me."

I rear my head back slightly. "What does that mean?"

He sighs. "It means, if it's okay with you, I'm okay with her having a relationship with Reese."

"I-I don't—" I stammer. "I don't understand."

"You said it yourself this morning," he states. "There's no such thing as being loved too much. And I don't want to deny Reese of that. Because the truth is, I have no doubt that my mother will, if she doesn't already, love Reese."

I mull over what he's saying, trying to work out how that makes *me* feel.

I know the woman has a lot of love to give, because that's what she gave me. And that is what I want to give other children who need that extra love and attention.

But I will forever struggle to reconcile the woman who welcomed me into her home and the woman who pushed her son out of his.

"There's going to have to be some stipulations," I say. "Surely, some more groveling. I don't want her thinking that she can just waltz back into our lives with a smile and an apology, and everything is okay."

"I completely agree," he assures. "No waltzing and no smiling. We'll take it slow and make sure she knows there is no relationship with Reese if Victoria and Dad aren't on board. I'm not ashamed to say we need their help to make this work, and if they can't help, then that's okay too," he explains. "And her having a relationship with Reese does not mean it's happy family times for her and us."

"And what about her and us?" I ask, treading carefully, wanting to cover all the bases. "I heard what you said after you asked her about the wedding."

Deacon brings his hands up to cup my face, lowering his mouth to mine. "I know where you belong." *Kiss.* "You know where I belong" *Kiss.* "Rhett knows where you belong." *Kiss.*

"You're my heart." *Kiss.* "My world." *Kiss.* "My love." *Kiss.* "Mine."

Feeling every bit his, I attach myself to him, his mouth on mine. My tongue licks at the seam of Deacon's lips, seeking entry, wanting more, wanting to taste him and claim him. Needing nothing more than the surety of his sweet declarations to subdue the jumble of nerves rioting beneath my skin. I kiss him and kiss him and kiss him and kiss him till a light bulb of an idea takes root in the back of my mind, and I can't help but drag my mouth off his and ask, "Does that mean you've changed your mind on how many children we show love to?"

It probably isn't the best time for me to bring this up, but we're under a time crunch, and I feel like his reference earlier to our conversation this morning has opened the door.

Chuckling, Deacon gives a slight shake of his head. "I see what you did there. Kiss me stupid and just see what you can get out of me?"

"Well?"

"I never said I only want one child," he clarifies. "I'm just scared about having two."

My head and shoulders sag momentarily, hating his rejection of the idea and knowing I have to accept and respect it. I know it's more than likely a timing issue than him being completely closed off to the idea. But the thought of turning this little boy away, brings back memories of *being* that little boy.

"But I know how much it means to you." Deacon places a finger beneath my chin and tips my head up so I'm looking at him again. "And I know how amazing you are at being a parent and a husband. And I know when it gets rough or rocky, you'll know how to walk us through."

"You're too good to me," I tell him, my gaze getting lost in his. "But I can wait. Unfortunately, there will be more children who need—"

"Julian," he interrupts. "I want to do this with you."

"You've dealt with a lot today. So many emotions," I ramble. "We can talk tomorrow."

"Julian," he repeats, his voice stern. "Today has been a perfect day"

This catches me off guard. "It has?"

"It has," he reiterates. "I started the day with a perfect husband and a perfect child, and I'm going to sleep with a perfect husband and maybe two perfect children."

PART 3

WITH YOU

DEACON

Eight Years Later

"**W**hat the hell is that?"

My eyes dart to the nightstand beside our bed and the five-minute timer that is suddenly displayed on my cell phone screen.

"What?" Julian's head peeks out from under the covers, where his head is resting awfully close to my very hard cock. "Our kids are going to roll up in here in five minutes, ten if we're lucky, wanting breakfast, and I would like to start the day with your dick in my mouth."

My body shakes as I laugh. "Well, I'm not opposed to it, but do we really need the timer?"

"Yes. If I can make you come in less than five minutes, I win."

"You win what?"

"Your cum down my throat."

"I'm not even going to pretend to understand your logic," I say. Grabbing the edge of the duvet, I throw it off of us to ensure I get a complete view of Julian, then reach over to start the timer. "But I'm not saying no to a morning blow job."

Julian's mouth wraps around me almost immediately and my hips arch up off the mattress, pushing me deeper down his throat. Determined to make time, I rest my hand on the back of his head, gripping his hair, and fuck his throat.

There is no finesse in my touch, nothing but hunger and need between us. This is how it is for us, stolen touches and rushed moments. We've learned the hard way that intimacy with rambunctious children who have no sense of personal space is pretty much non-existent. That means, every now and then Julian and I needed to get a little bit creative, and while it's usually Julian who gets carried away, I always go along for the ride.

With urgency and fervor, Julian's mouth bobs up and down my length. He cradles my sac in his palm, massaging each ball, before dipping under and applying pressure to my taint. It's the perfect combination, every touch and suck, bringing me closer to the edge.

"I'm going to come," I announce as I glance at the timer that shows we have a whole two minutes left. My hips piston into Julian's mouth, and he takes it, every short and sharp thrust.

It's brutal and aggressive and so very desperate, but after fifteen years together, ten of those married, eight of them with two kids, I'm just grateful that every part of him still wants every part of me.

My muscles tighten as he continues to take me to the back of his throat, and the sound of him gagging on my cock has my body ready to explode.

"Fuck, baby. You're so good at that," I praise. "I'm right fucking there. Right. Fucking. There."

My orgasm barrels through me, the rush and speed of it all making it almost impossible to catch my breath. My chest heaves as Julian climbs up over me. I watch him push the waistband of his boxer briefs beneath his balls, freeing his erection, before slamming his mouth down on mine.

Knowing what he needs, I wrap my hands around his dick and jerk him, hard and fast. My tongue feasts on his, the salty taste of myself adding to the carnality of it all. It's a race to the finish line now, and I know we'll both do anything to make it.

My cell vibrates atop the nightstand just as Julian comes apart in my hand and all over my chest. Time is up.

Heavy breaths fill the air as Julian's gaze darts between the mess on my chest and my face. He smears his fingers through his cum, rubbing it into my skin, just as I bring my own hand to my mouth and lick up every drop of his arousal. It's filthy and possessive, and the most perfect way to start our day.

Instead of revelling in the afterglow like I want to, we both move like a well-oiled machine, getting cleaned up in record time, only to realize Reese still hasn't barged into our bedroom like she does every morning, and now I'm starting to worry.

"They're not still asleep, are they?" I ask Julian.

I open the bedroom door in a hurry, only to come to a complete stop when I see Reese holding a huge, decorated poster board that says "Happy ten year anniversary!" in big neon colored letters. Her dark-blonde hair is in a braid, and she's still dressed in her pink plaid patterned pajamas.

"Sweetheart," I say, the smile on my face widening by the millisecond. "How long have you been standing here?"

"Maybe five minutes." Her chocolate-colored gaze darts past me. "Is that right, Daddy?"

Julian comes up behind me, wrapping his arms around my waist. "That sounds about right."

I glance at him over my shoulder. "What's this? Are you in on this?"

He kisses me quickly on the cheek before murmuring into my ear, "All I was told was to keep you busy this morning. And I think I did a *really* good job."

I chuckle as Reese hands Julian the anniversary sign, then slips her small hand into mine. She leads me to the kitchen where the sight of Rowan flipping pancakes has my heart wanting to burst right through my chest.

At twelve years old he's growing into such an amazing young man. Already five foot two, he's tall and forever growing. It's hard to think eight years have passed since Julian and I walked into that hospital room to meet him for the very first time. Naturally, it wasn't an easy road for any of us. Navigating grief in a four-and-a-half-year-old wasn't for the faint hearted, but our own experiences made me feel like we were somehow the perfect fit for him.

"Morning, bud," I say as I walk toward him and kiss him on the top of his head. "These look great."

"Thanks," he murmurs shyly. "I know they're your favorite."

I kiss him again and squeeze his shoulder, the bittersweet feeling of watching him grow up sitting like a constant ache in my chest. I'm eager for him to grow and experience the world and gain independence, but I often miss the days where he didn't want to do anything without me.

"Okay, Dad, you have to sit here." Reese tugs on my hand, ushering me to one side of the table and then Julian to the other. "And, Daddy, you sit here."

Julian and I wear matching smiles as we dutifully obey

our daughter and watch her excitedly receive instructions from Rowan on how to set the table for our anniversary breakfast.

The bond between them makes me feel like Rowan entering our lives was kismet. We took the time to learn him while he took the time to learn her. His love language is acts of service, and there isn't a day that passes, where he doesn't show Reese just how much he loves her.

He's patient and protective in a way that reminds me that your family is beyond what you were born into, it's beyond blood and beyond lineage, and very much blossoms from the simpler, more overlooked things in life: love, adoration, and respect.

And Reese is young enough that he's always been her older brother. What started out as a semi-permanent placement, turned into us adopting Rowan, because the thought of him leaving any of us was too much to bear.

It isn't easy, as any parent knows, but eventually they start talking and walking and feeding themselves, and your job as a parent shifts from milestone to milestone, back and forth, teacher to friend, friend to teacher.

"Are you sure you two don't need any help?" Julian offers. "I can make coffee and hot chocolate for everyone."

"No," she says adamantly. "You and Dad can clean up since Rowan and I set the table and cooked."

Julian digs his teeth into his bottom lip, hiding his smile. "Not a problem. Your Dad and I will clean up."

"And Row knows how to make hot chocolate, don't you Row?"

Turning the stove off, Rowan picks up the plate of hot, fresh pancakes and strides toward the table. "Yeah, Pa showed me how."

Julian and I decided early on that we didn't really care

what the kids called us. Between the both of them, either one of us has been Dad, Dads, Papa, Daddy, or Pa. They use them all on rotation, and we respond to each of them. But over time, Rowan has gravitated to calling me Dad and Julian Pa, but even without the distinction, we each have an individual connection with each child, that no matter the moniker, you know from the sound of their voice which parent they need in that moment.

"See," she chirps proudly. "Rowan can make it."

"Come on," I say, gesturing for them to sit down. "I would much rather you both eat the food before it gets cold. I'll plate up everyone's pancakes and your dad can make everyone's drink of choice."

Reese isn't too impressed with my disruption to her celebratory breakfast, but she listens to me and sits down anyway. While I'm so grateful for their thoughtfulness, I want to take care of them. It's my job and my purpose, Julian and parenthood giving me a sense of steadfastness I didn't know I would or could ever experience.

"How many do you both want?" I ask them as I put one on each of their plates.

"There's enough for all of us to have four each," Rowan informs me. Which is code for *please give everyone four*. So, despite knowing Reese won't be able to finish four, and Rowan will eat her leftovers, I stack each person's plate four pancakes high.

Julian returns to the table only a few minutes later, placing down a drink in front of each child, only to duck back to the kitchen and grab a coffee for each of us and a thick white envelope I've never seen before.

Julian places it in front of me and then sets my mug of coffee beside my plate of pancakes.

"What's this?" I ask, raising it to my face.

"Open it," Reese shouts enthusiastically, making Rowan laugh.

Sliding my finger under the flap, I try and fail to open it without tearing it. "Shit."

"Dad. That's a bad word," Reese hisses.

"Sorry," I drawl.

I drag the rectangle-shaped cardboard out of the envelope and turn it over to see what looks like a wedding invitation.

"Isn't this our wedding invitation?" I can feel my forehead crease in confusion as I glance up to look at Julian, who is standing beside me. "What am I missing?"

"Look again," Rowan says.

My gaze dances over the words, finally noticing the small and subtle differences.

Deacon and Julian Reid-Sutton invite you to their ten-year anniversary party.

"We're having a party? Tonight?" I exclaim.

"Pa wanted it to be a surprise," Rowan informs me. "But I told him you wouldn't like it, because you and I are the same and we hate being the center of attention."

Emotion lodges itself in my throat at hearing him point out our similarities. Something about him wanting to connect us, always stealing my breath.

"You're right." My voice cracks as I catch his gaze. "Thank you for telling him."

"And I'm going to be the flower girl," Reese announces. "And Rowan is going to be your best man."

Looking over my shoulder, I smile at Julian. "You really thought of everything."

He tips his head toward the kids as he moves around the table and takes his seat. "It was all their idea."

Sliding the invitation back into the envelope, I move it

off to the side and encourage everyone to start eating before the food gets any colder. And just like I predicted, it's no time before Reese is holding her belly at one and a half pancakes and Rowan is on to his sixth.

"Dad," Reese whines. "Can we give Daddy his present now?"

Julian's head snaps up. "I thought we said no presents?"

"Hi, pot. Meet kettle."

He rolls his eyes at me, and I turn to face the kids. "Reese, you know where it is. You want to go get it?"

She hops down off the dining table chair. "There's an extra two boxes, be sure to bring them too."

Excited, Reese skips down the hallway and into our home office. She comes back into view only moments later, walking carefully as she holds the presents in her small hands.

Passing them to me, I return one to her, give one to Rowan, then rise up off my chair and hand the last one to Julian.

Before I can turn to leave, he grabs my hand and keeps me standing next to him. Realizing I have the perfect view, I slowly scan my gaze over the three of them as they each open their present.

Rowan whips his head up in confusion, just as I hear Julian's breath hitch.

"You bought us gloves." Julian's correct observation steals my attention. Pushing his chair out, he leaps into my arms, giving me only a fraction of a second to catch him. I hold him against me as he whispers over and over, "You bought us gloves."

"The weather is getting colder, and you're due for some new ones," I explain, pretending I don't know after all these years just how significant the simple gesture is. In the moment, he was cold, and I wanted to make sure he kept warm. In the grand scheme of things, Julian knows there isn't anything I wouldn't give him.

It doesn't matter if it's small or big, hard or easy.

"You bought us gloves," he repeats. "For Reese and Rowan and Me."

Looking around the room, I see how Rowan and Reese watch us with intense concentration, always curious about the life we lived before them.

"You're my family," I tell him. "And I buy my family gloves."

JULIAN

The party is in full swing, our backyard decorated with a marquee, tables and chairs, and gas heaters to warm up the guests. It's a lot, over the top even, especially for Deacon and me, but Rowan and Reese are eating it up.

We decided against the formality of a ceremony or an aisle, splurged on the food and drinks, and made sure there would be dancing.

A few months ago, we were going through photos and video footage of our wedding and Reese offhandedly said, "I wish we were there, Daddy."

And an idea was born.

Looking like a princess, Reese is absolutely breathtaking in a beautiful ivory satin dress that has a gorgeous puffy skirt. While Rowan's suit matches mine and Deacon's.

I know tonight will be a night they will both remember fondly. In a way that I could not explain, both our kids are in love with our love. And I don't know if it's because we love loud and proud or because we make them feel safe enough to love loud and proud too.

While Reese is outgoing, Rowan is reserved, they

complement one another beautifully. Reese is affectionate and tactile in her love, and Rowan is the young man who notices how many balls you're juggling everyday and takes it upon himself to do everyone's laundry just to make it easier.

And they're both what the other needs, always coaxing the other out of their shell. Like siblings often do, they alternate between being a figurative punching bag and a support pillow for one another.

"What are you doing?" Victoria moves in beside me, handing me a glass of champagne.

"Just ogling your brother," I say truthfully.

"It's the kids, isn't it?" she says. "When Hayden is in dad mode, I just wanna fuck his brains out."

I laugh at her candidness, chuckling a little bit harder, because she's right, it's the kids. But it's also that only a few hours ago, I was sliding a two-inch-long, black, silicone butt plug into Deacon's tight ass, because that's exactly what I wanted to do: Fuck his brains out.

Steering my thoughts away from anything that'll encourage an erection in public, I focus on Deacon and the way he's holding Reese's hand. With his other arm protectively slung across Rowan's shoulders, he looks so relaxed and content, laughing and talking to our friends, with our kids by his side.

I thought the pride I felt ten years ago at finally being married to the love of my life would be unrivaled, but watching him parent and love our children so effortlessly outweighed it every time.

I watch as Deacon casually peruses the yard, subtly trying to look for me while staying engaged in the conversation. I wait for his gaze to land on mine, and when it does, the sexiest smile spreads across his face.

He's nearing forty-five years old, and looking at him still makes my heart stutter and my body light up like a live wire. He has a smattering of gray on his temples and in his beard, making him look both distinguished and sexy. And laugh lines at the corners of his eyes and mouth that I enjoyed putting there.

Tipping his chin up at me, he gestures for me to join him.

"Come on," I say, grabbing Victoria's elbow and bringing her with me. "Your brother's wish is my command."

"Twenty-year-old me would've said you two are so gross," Victoria says as we walk. "But almost-fifty-year-old me is so unbelievably proud of you both."

"Does drinking still make you emotional?" I tease.

"Shut up," she says, nudging my shoulder. "I was trying to be nice."

"I know," I assure her. "I'm proud of us too."

We head over to Deacon, who shifts over just enough for me to slide in between him and Reese, while Victoria has other ideas. I watch her whisper in Hayden's ear, and I catch the smirk on Hayden's face that follows.

Giving me a wink, she hightails it out of there and into the house, with her husband hot on her heels.

"I don't even want to know what that was about," Deacon murmurs against the shell of my ear.

A chuckle rumbles in my chest as I take a good look around at the people who showed up for us a second time.

We're standing between a large group of our friends, those we've spent the last ten years or more living and loving with. Finding their own way and growing their own families, it's a testament to the strength and importance of found family.

Those people in your life who stayed for the long haul, swam with you and beside you through the surf and through the still.

"Julian," Wade greets. "Just the man I've been looking for. I'm kinda bummed you didn't want me to revive my time as a wedding officiant for the night."

"I figured you might like that it's a little bit less stressful this time around," I reply lightheartedly. "If I remember correctly, there was an hour of time where you had lost our wedding rings."

"'Lost' is a strong word," he says in defense. "I misplaced them. And then I found out Christie was keeping them safe, so that hardly really counts because she and I are basically the same person."

"He's right," our friend Gael chimes in. "My parents speak to Jordan and me like we're interchangeable and it's a full time job keeping up."

A subtle tugging on my arm shifts my attention away from the conversation. I glance down at Reese expectantly, certain I know what she's about to ask before the words even leave her mouth.

"Can we have cake now?" she whispers

Slipping her hand in mine, I give it a little squeeze. "Do you think we can wait for half an hour or so?"

Biting her bottom lip, she mulls it over before nodding in defeat. "Can I at least find Emilia and show her the new art set in my room?"

I tip my head to Gael and Jordan. "If it's okay with her dads, then it's fine with me."

We all watch Reese sweet talk her way with Jordan and Gael as Jesse says, "I remember when Raine was like that. It was about the age she was when she met Leo." He glances lovingly at his husband. "And she had him wrapped around her finger from the get go. She would talk to him with her cute, sugary voice and she got whatever she wanted."

With permission from Gael and Jordan, we all watch Reese excitedly run off to find their daughter Emilia. At the same time, Rowan uses that as his cue to walk away from us and dutifully follow his sister. He never lets her out of his sight, and for now it works in our favor.

"Sorry we're late." Familiar voices have ten sets of eyes darting their way.

Both wearing black slacks and dress shirts with their sleeves rolled up, it's impossible to miss the bronze-like glow that radiates off them.

"I could've sworn you two were in Australia," Deacon says as both men move around the circle, shaking everyone's hands.

"We were," Pierce answers. "We got back this morning."

"And let me guess, after a million hours on a plane, the first place you wanted to be was here," Deacon jokes as Pierce leans into him for a hug.

"Definitely that," Pierce says. "Or maybe this was a good way to combat the jet lag."

"User," I murmur jokingly as we greet one another hello. "Seriously though, how was Australia?"

"The surf is no fucking joke," Auden says as he shakes my hand and leans in for a hug. "And the kangaroos. We went to some beautiful beaches and, holy shit, they're just out there hopping around, minding their business. And they're so huge, some of them were easily as tall as Pierce and me."

The conversation continues, Auden and Pierce sharing more about their trip, only for someone to go off on a tangent that everyone follows.

Being around everyone, my cup is full, my chest is about to burst with just how happy I am in this moment, and I don't know if I want to laugh or cry. My mind takes me back to that twenty-six-year-old man, lying on his bed in a suit, crippled with grief, crying his eyes out.

You couldn't have told me that this is where my life would be all these years later. And if you did, I wouldn't believe you. Because there is no way one man could be this lucky.

No way I could be this lucky.

"Pa." Rowan's voice pulls me out of the past, his green eyes wide and staring up at me. "Can I talk to you and Dad for a second?"

The crease forming between his brows is a dead give-away that something is bothering him. "What is it, Row?"

Deacon's hand finds the small of my back, his body shifting closer, clearly paying attention to Rowan's distress. "Let's go inside," he says, his voice taking on that protective but authoritarian tone.

Wading through the guests, the three of us make our way inside, bypassing the kitchen and Deacon's parents, and head to Rowan's room.

Closing the door, I turn to find Rowan sitting on the edge of the bed and Deacon standing beside him.

"What's wrong?" Deacon asks him. "Did something happen?"

"No." Rowan shakes his head. "I didn't mean to worry you, but..." His words are replaced by a heavy sigh. "I don't want to say a speech in front of everyone tonight."

"What?" Deacon turns to look at me, clearly confused. "What speech?"

Before I have a chance to fill him in, Rowan's explaining what we had planned to Deacon. "Reese wanted us to say our own vows. Like, not to one another." He rolls his eyes, as if to say obviously. "She wanted us to say all the things we love about you and Pa."

I can't help but steal a glance at Deacon, whose mouth is curling up at the side in a small smile just like mine. We're truly the luckiest men alive.

"But I don't want to say all that stuff in front of everyone," he reiterates. "Dad, you know I hate being the center of attention."

His eyes dart to Deacon, needing the solidarity, and Deacon gifts it to him effortlessly. "You don't have to do anything you don't want to do."

"But I do want to do it," Rowan insists.

"Just not in front of everyone," I finish for him.

He nods vehemently. "I just don't want to let Reese down. She's so excited."

A knock on the door interrupts us.

"Rowww it's me," Reese cries emphatically. "Open up."

"Is it okay if she comes in?" I ask, wanting to make sure we're validating his feelings and not prematurely railroading him with hers.

Wordlessly, he strides to the door and opens it up, very obviously answering my question. Space is not an issue for these two.

I'm surprised when I see Deacon's parents on the other side of the door behind Reese.

"Sorry," Elaine says. "She was distraught looking for him." Her hands stroking Reese's hair, she says, "Look, sweetheart, he's here. Everything is fine."

It had been eight years since we let Elaine back into our lives, and it's been an interesting journey to say the least. I'd personally expected push back after we explained what was required in order to have a relationship with our children, but Elaine respected our boundaries in a way that surprised both Deacon and me.

Words and feelings are not her strong suit and neither is being able to admit defeat. To this day, she has truly never really elaborated or explained when it comes to apologizing to Deacon. But her actions toward Reese and Rowan are those of a changed woman, a humbled woman, an apologetic woman.

And while things still have never been the same between her and Deacon and me, every now and then, like tonight, the walls come down for the sake of the kids.

"What if we do it in here?" Rowan suggests excitedly, looking at Reese. "And then we'll go and eat cake."

"Do what in here?" Deacon asks, thoroughly confused.

"Our vows," Rowan says. "Or your vows. Our family vows?"

His confusion at this makes me laugh, his always-so-serious nature coming through.

"It's our day," I remind him. "You, Me, Reese, and Dad. That's the only thing that matters."

"Can I at least say them in here and when we cut the cake?" Reese asks.

Looking over them, and at Deacon, I shake my head. "I fear this whole idea has become bigger than I intended."

Smirking, he shrugs. "Can never have enough love, right?"

"You need a t-shirt, at this point."

He chews at the corner of his lip. "The t-shirt is not on my priority list right now."

I drag my gaze up and down the length of his body, loving the simple flush in his cheeks. It reminds me so much of us in the wedding suite on our actual wedding day, and just like now, we're volleying between heat and heart at every turn.

"Okay, I'm going to start," Deacon says, glancing around the room, his voice loud. "Rowan and Reese. I promise to love you both unconditionally."

Reese immediately shoots her hand up in the air. "I promise to never lie."

"That's a good start," I murmur through a smile. "Rowan?"

"I promise to love you all unconditionally."

My throat bobs at his words, words that weigh heavy and have so much meaning, more than his twelve-year-old heart knows, and my eyes can't help but move to Elaine and Bill. "Do you want a turn?" I ask her.

"Yes, Grandma," Reese says excitedly. "Have a turn."

Her gaze darts between the two kids before landing on Deacon. "I promise to listen and learn."

I catch the slight nod Deacon gives her, his expression full of appreciation and understanding, before turning his attention to me.

With Reese's and Rowan's eyes wide in excitement, I opt for something light hearted to keep the momentum going. "I promise to always share my chocolate with you." I point at each of them. "All of you."

"Me too!" Reese shouts. "And I promise to always make my bed."

"This is the best idea you two have had yet," Deacon says. "What about emptying the dishwasher and putting away the laundry?"

Rowan pulls out a piece of paper from his pocket. "I have those on my list too."

This kid is too damn cute.

"Why don't you read it out to us," Bill steps into the

room and suggests, probably anticipating just how long this will take if we let these two run the show. And Deacon and I almost always let them run the show.

"Reese, honey, do you have a list too?" he adds.

Rowan pulls out another piece of paper and hands it to her. "I kept it so she doesn't lose it."

"Okay, let's all find a comfortable place to sit and then you two read them to your dads"

Between the bed, the desk chair, and the floor, we spread ourselves around the room, and they read out their lists.

There are almost fifty promises between them and counting, And even though we have a whole house full of friends and family, there isn't a single place in the world any of us would rather be.

Their list ranges from helping us around the house to making sure they never go to sleep angry at one another. Their lists are so well thought out, I'm in awe, but I also don't expect anything less from either of them.

I can't confidently say it's us, because it isn't true. It takes a village to raise children, even an occasionally dysfunctional one like ours, and everything they've learned —their love, their empathy, their compassion—has been taught to them by all of us. Including Elaine and Bill.

"Okay, it's time for our last one," Reese announces.

Rowan looks down at his list and then looks between Deacon and me.

"We promise to clean up after our dog," he says.

"And take it for walks," says Reese.

"And teach it how to sit and shake hands."

"Wait," Deacon says, shaking his head. "What are you two talking about? We don't have a dog." He looks up at me. "Did you buy us a dog?"

"No!" I exclaim. "I'm just as confused as you are."

"Don't look at us," Elaine says, putting her hands up in surrender. "We spoil them, but a dog seems like a recipe for disaster."

"We don't have a dog," Row says, a cautious smile on his face. "But can we get one?"

Reese stands in the middle of the room, batting her big, childlike doe eyes. "It can be our anniversary present." She puts her hands together like she's praying. "Please."

AFTER DEACON and I stopped laughing with the kids at just how wrapped around their fingers they both have us, Reese made a unanimous decision—it was cake time and then she was ready for her and Rowan's sleep over at Elaine and Bill's place.

"Julian and I just want to thank you all for coming here tonight and celebrating our wedding anniversary," Deacon says to all our friends. "It feels like it was only yesterday I was walking down the aisle. Life seemed so full of promise, and when I look around this room..." His gaze lands on Row, Reese, and me, the three of us standing huddled beside him. "Life more than delivered."

Clapping and cheering fill the yard as Deacon comes closer to us, kissing both Rowan and Reese on the head as they pass us by to enjoy dessert with their friends.

"I love you," he says. Reaching for me, he intertwines our fingers and tugs me close, our bodies flush against one another. "And I love all these people."

Arms wrapped around my neck, he kisses me softly. "But how about instead of promising to share your chocolate with me, you make me another one."

"Yeah?" I say with a teasing tone. "Promise you what?"

Kissing me again, he subtly grazes his hips against mine, and I can feel his cock thickening against me. "Promise me that this'll be over soon."

"I promise," I say against his lips.

"Promise me we will worry about cleaning up tomorrow."

Laughing, because it's a hard ask, I sneak a hand down to his ass and squeeze. "I promise."

Deacon kisses me along my jaw until his mouth is below my ear, his voice low enough only I can hear him. "Promise you'll replace this plug with your cock."

"I promise."

"Promise you'll make love to me."

My hand still on his ass, I push him into me, my length against his. "I promise."

"And fuck my brains out."

A gravelly chuckle leaves my mouth. "Definitely."

He rears his head back to lock his eyes with mine. "Make me yours?"

"Always," I promise.

Only him and me.

Me and him.

Husbands.

ROWAN

Fifteen Years Later

The repetitive vibrations are a dead giveaway I'm receiving a flurry of texts. And the flurry of texts are a dead giveaway that my sister's name is filling up the screen. Feeling slow and sluggish after last night, I sit up, the bedsheet falling to my waist, and grab my cell off the rickety table beside my bed.

Just like I anticipated, Reese is on a rampage.

> I know why you're staying away.
>
> I respect it. Understand it even.
>
> I know how hurt you are.
>
> But it's their twenty-fifth wedding anniversary, Row.
>
> And I need you to come home.
>
> Rowan
>
> Rowan

ROWAN!

Geez, Reese. Dramatic much?

Just making sure you're reading my messages.

Me: I'm reading them.

And?

And what?

Rowan Reid-Sutton!!!

A dainty arm curls around my torso. "Come back to bed," she drawls. "It's too early to be awake."

Sighing, I drop my head between my shoulders. "It's over, Emilia. I have to go home."

Did I just hint at a Second Generation Novel?

Until then, do you want more Deacon and Julian?
Visit
https://www.marleyvbooks.com/bonus-epilogues
to have a With You Bonus scene delivered straight to your kindle.

Did you enjoy meeting Deacon and Julian's friends?

To read about Jesse and Leo in What We Broke, visit Amazon.

To read about Gael and Jordan in Ache, visit Amazon.

To read about Auden and Pierce in Want You Still, visit Amazon.

ACKNOWLEDGMENTS

Thank you Julian and Deacon for pulling me out of an almost twelve month no writing slump.

Thank you to Steph, Kacey, Laura, Tanya, Jodi, Beth, Sybil and Shauna for keeping me sane and on track.

And thank you to you, for always showing up and reading my books.

Until we do it all again.

Much Peace and Love.

ABOUT THE AUTHOR

Living in Sydney, Australia with her family, Marley Valentine is a USA Today bestselling author and a former social worker who uses her past experiences to write real life, emotional and heartfelt contemporary romance.

She enjoys writing many queer dynamics, incorporating all forms of life, lust and love as her characters embark on their journey to their happily ever after.

When she's not busy writing her own stories, she spends most of her time immersed in the words of her favourite authors.

Marley enjoys interacting with her readers so please feel free to reach out to her via Facebook, Instagram, email and/or subscribe to her newsletter.

Other Books by Marley Valentine

Reclaim | Revive | Rectify

MM Romance Books

Devilry | Without You | Ache | Unforgettable (Vino & Veritas) | What We Broke | Want You Still

<u>**The Unlucky Ones**</u>

<u>**Unwanted**</u> | <u>**Unloved**</u> | <u>**Unlikely**</u>

Find Marley

www.marleyvbooks.com